International editions sold for EPIC and SAGA:
The United States of America, Canada,
Australia, New Zealand, Asia,
South Africa, Germany, Russia,
France, Czech Republic, Ukraine,
Portugal, Brazil, Italy, Serbia and Denmark.

CONOR KOSTICK was a designer for the world's first live fantasy role-playing game, based in Peckforton Castle, Cheshire. He lives in Dublin where he teaches medieval history at Trinity College Dublin. He is the author of several historical, political and cultural works. Conor was also a reviewer for the *Journal of Music in Ireland* and was twice chairperson of the Irish Writers' Union. He co-wrote *The Easter Rising: A Guide to Dublin in 1916*, and co-edited *Irish Writers Against War*, an anthology of writings by Irish authors in response to the war in Iraq.

Epic (2004) and *Saga* (2006), two fantasy futuristic novels by Conor Kostick have received great acclaim worldwide.

Move

Conor Kostick

THE O'BRIEN PRESS
DUBLIN

First published 2008
by The O'Brien Press Ltd.
12 Terenure Road East,
Dublin 6, Ireland.
Tel: +353 1 4923333
Fax: +353 1 4922777
E-mail: books@obrien.ie
Website: www.obrien.ie

ISBN 978-1-84717-010-1

British Library Cataloguing-in-Publication Data
A catalogue record for this title is available from the British Library

The O'Brien Press
receives assistance from

1 2 3 4 5 6
08 09 10 11 12

Editing, typesetting and design: The O'Brien Press Ltd
Printed and bound in the UK by J.H. Haynes & Co Ltd, Sparkford.

For Aoife
And the new realms you show me

Contents

1

Blue Plastic Sandals

The first time I 'moved', I had no control over it. It wasn't long after my fourteenth birthday and my class were on a school trip: a journey along a canal. Our barge was puttering through the murky water, full of merry exuberant kids. We loved the fact that Miss Day was cooking sausages in a pan over a little gas fire and making us all hot dogs in the outdoors. It was a bright sunny day and I was happy.

Then, like a premonition, a mosquito landed on the soft inside of my arm. A moment later it bent over and bit me, the bag of its body quickly swelling up with my blood. I ignored the sting; it was fascinating to see the fly change, filling its body before jumping off, bloated and twice as heavy as when it had landed.

The soft coughing of another engine made me look up. A barge, painted vividly in white and red, was coming our way. The man at the tiller was smiling at our rowdy boat and touched his hat to us. In response to his wave, our boat steered to the left and, as a result, came close to the wide flat stones that paved the sides of the canal. This gave the girls up the front the opportunity to mess about. Some of them jumped across from the wooden frame of our barge to the bank.

One of the smaller girls in our class, Tara, stood up to have a go, and stumbled. Just as she fell, hitting her shins on the stone lip of the canal wall, our boat closed up the gap. We felt a shudder from the impact of the barge against the canal wall and there was a loud crack, like someone had broken a dry stick across their knee.

It all happened right in front of me. The inexorable momentum of the barge was causing the vessel to grind along the wall, right across Tara's foot. She was white, utterly white, and she looked across into my eyes. There was a kind of pleading in her face, as if to ask 'it's not true, is it?' But I looked down at her leg and threw up in an uncontrollable spasm. By doing so, it was as if I'd failed her. She knew it was true.

As the barge came away from the wall there were screams from the others, who could now see what had happened. Tara's foot was broken, but it wasn't just broken. It was horrible. Scarlet blood was streaming down the stones of the canal wall, but that wasn't the worst of it. The worst thing was the sight of a pathetically sad little blue plastic sandal hanging loose below the crushed foot.

A moment later, Tara screamed.

Hopefully you've never heard anyone really scream. Of course you'll have heard shrieks and stuff, even fairly serious screams, like those from the other girls on the canal bank. But this was something else; this was as if all the horror and pain of the whole world was howling in your ears. It paralysed me and made me curl up, shrinking inside myself to avoid the terrible sound.

It was the screaming that pushed me over the edge. I just wanted to escape, to be anywhere else, not to be standing there, unable to look away, and listening to screams that clawed through my whole body.

* * *

When I woke up, I saw my mum leaning over me.

'Mum? Where am I?'

She laughed. 'Home, silly.'

It was true. I was lying in my own bed. The screams had faded fast. Somewhere I knew they were still continuing, but thankfully not here. The clock read 3.35.

'What about the canal trip?'

'That left long ago. Don't you remember? You were too sick to go.'

Now that she drew my attention to it, I could remember getting up, then feeling a bit dizzy. The fact that I hadn't eaten any breakfast was noticed by my mum, as was my slightly dazed behaviour. That's right. It was coming back more strongly now.

She'd placed a cool hand against my head, and then taken my temperature. Much as I'd wanted to go on the trip, I'd agreed to go back to bed.

Was the accident all just a feverish dream? Writing about it now, that's the obvious conclusion anyone would have come to. Except that I knew it hadn't been a dream. I had been there, really been there, until just a few minutes ago and it was absolutely nothing like a dream.

Did you ever see a drawing where if you just look at the black lines, you see something, say birds, but when you look at the white parts of the drawing, you see something else, like a face? Both pictures are there at the same time, but you can't fix on them simultaneously, you have to see one or the other. Well it was like that with my memories, only they were not black and white, but a rich composition of bright colours, sounds, tastes, scents. And screams.

There was no way I was going back to the barge, even if I could have. I settled into my bed and into this version of the world, with the other version receding and fading, like I'd walked out of a dark cinema, back into the daylight, and begun to forget the horror film I'd just seen.

There was something else. I knew, even then, what I'd done was wrong. The more moral reader will have already noticed that my wish had been a selfish one. I hadn't wished that Tara was uninjured; I'd simply wished to get away from the barge. That's true and that's the way I was back then. There's not many of my classmates would have been different either. It's how most people are in an emergency. But the fact that my desire to escape had been selfish wasn't what was troubling me.

A lingering sensation that I had done something wrong, perhaps injured someone, lay heavy upon me. But who? Why did I feel like I was inside the mind of a shark that had just scented blood? Whatever I had done was repulsive, but at the same time it was exciting. To be fair to the young lad who moved away from that horrific scene, I didn't know what I'd done and I certainly didn't know how to fix it.

While I was deep in thought, feeling my way around the strangely split memories, the buzzing of my phone made me jump. It was a text from my best mate, Zed.

'OMG. Total Chaos. Taras leg knackered. Hsptl. Blud. Jamie waz sic. All the girlz r crying. U missed it all!'

Looking at the little black letters on the phone's screen, I shuddered. The echo of that scream was ringing in my head. I could see it all again. But it wasn't just the recollection of that awful moment that made me shiver. Zed's text proved it wasn't a dream. It was true. Some kind of magic, some kind of unnatural magic, had taken place. And I had caused it to happen.

What would you have done next? I was tempted to tell my mum. Even though it was so unbelievable, I could prove it; I could describe exactly what had happened, what everyone was wearing, who was standing where. But I didn't. Partly it was because of that guilty feeling, for some reason I felt like I'd done something she would be angry about. It was also because my mum was worried that I was a bit more geeky and soft than other kids. She was always at me to go out and play in the street, rather than be on the computer. Trying to describe this to her would be risky. She'd probably think I was going mad. Maybe I was?

What I did do was wait until she left the room. Then I rang Zed.

'Liam, Jays' man, what a day.'

'Where are you Zed?'

'On the bus.'

'Can you call up to me when you're home?'

'Sure, as soon as we're back.'

'Thanks Zed.'

'Later.'

***

It was about an hour later that I heard the doorbell ring.

'Zed wants to come up. Is that all right?' asked my mum.

'Sure.'

Zed is a bit like Tigger in the Winnie the Pooh stories. Well, an Asian-looking Tigger, with a taste for heavy metal. When he enters a room he bounds in full of energy and immediately becomes the centre of attention. What most of my class never realised about him was that he has a lot of respect for brains and he never sneered at me like some of the others did. That's why we were mates. That, and the fact that for years he lived right across the road from me.

'Liam, man, it was incredible. Wait while I tell you.'

'Stop, stop right there Zed. I want to prove something to

you, something totally weird.'

He stopped.

'Hold on a second. We need some background noise.' I put on the radio, which had a channel preset to Kerrang! for when Zed visited.

'Yeah?'

'OK. This is really strange, kinda scary. But I was there all day on the barge and then when the accident happened, something magic happened and it was as if I'd never gone on the trip.'

'Erm, Liam, mate, you've been sick, like. You dreamt it.'

'Just listen.' And for the next ten minutes I told him how it was, all the while trying to read his face. Sometimes Zed looked surprised and sombre, at other times he shook his head.

'Well?' I asked him.

'I dunno. You weren't talking to anyone else?'

'No.'

He picked up my mobile phone and checked. I let him.

'Well, it's strange all right. Some of what you said is dead on and I don't see how you could make it up. But you said we had sausages just before the accident?'

'Yes.'

'Nah, mate, we had burgers.'

'Oh.'

'And she knackered her left foot?'

'Yes.'

Zed shook his head. 'Right.'

'That's really strange.' I was surprised. It was impossible to make sense of this information. Not that it would have been much better if my memories had been in total accord with Zed's view of what had happened. 'So close, but not quite the same. But you do agree about the clothes she was wearing? About what Miss Day was wearing? That earlier, at the start, Jocelyn had nearly fallen in, messing about at the back? And she was made to help with the food?'

'Yeah.'

He spoke reluctantly, but I felt hugely relieved. It meant that I wasn't going mad, that all this wasn't just happening in my head. Something really strange had happened to me today.

'There's this other thing as well.'

'Yeah?'

'I feel I shouldn't have done it. If it was magic, it wasn't good magic.'

'Magic? Do you think it was magic?' He was disbelieving.

'No. I'm just saying. It was like I was using some power in my head. But I shouldn't have. I've upset something. It's really hard to describe. I dunno. It's very confusing.'

'No kidding.' Zed widened his eyes. 'Can you do it again, though? Like now?'

'What? Get away from here to somewhere else?'

'Yeah.'

I thought about this and hadn't got a clue how I'd escaped from the barge in the first place.

'I don't think so.'

'What if I shriek my head off?' Zed smiled, making a joke out of it, but I shuddered.

'Yeah. Yeah, if it was for real, maybe that would do it. It has to be an emergency, I reckon.'

'Nice skill to have, mate.'

'So you believe me?'

'I think you had a vision or something, a flash of something in your head.'

'Should I tell my mum?'

'No way, Liam. If I was you I wouldn't tell anyone. They'll think you're a looper.'

'But you don't think I'm a looper?'

He looked at me for a long time.

'I've always thought you were a total madzer.'

2

Learning to 'Move'

After that, even though the whole experience was never far from my thoughts, I just got on with things. What else could I do? All the time I was alert for it happening again, but the only sign I'd ever moved was that I'd sometimes get nightmares in which Tara broke her foot. The strange thing about those dreams was that I didn't experience any of the horror, fear and sickness that I'd felt when it had happened for real. Actually, having those dreams was weirdly satisfying.

Being back in class with Tara was strange at first. It was like we had some kind of bond. At least, from my point of view it was. If it hadn't have been for her, this peculiar, dark, magic would never have happened. From her perspective though, we had no relationship at all. I hadn't even been there on the day of her accident. It's not surprising then, that when she caught me glancing at her, she looked back, blankly, not even curious. Perhaps I should have talked to her, but what could I say that wouldn't sound crazy? It wasn't as if I had any idea what had happened to me.

Not until nearly a year later did things begin to make a bit more sense. Because there then came a moment when I learned that I could move at will, that it wasn't just some bizarre magical thing that affected me in emergencies.

The school soccer 'C' team only played on days when Mr O'Connor, our P.E. teacher, had fixtures that could not be met by the 'A' and 'B' teams. This was only about four times a season. The 'C' team was a collection of players who had more enthusiasm for the sport than ability. We were misfits, not even friends with each other. But still, some masochistic bent in each of us would get us on to the cold field to be thrashed by a rival school.

Back then I wasn't the person I am now. I was shy; I preferred books to the babble of my classmates. My circle of friends was small. At that age I was the sort of kid that when you come, years later, to look at the picture of your former fourth-year class, you puzzle over it. What was the name of that geeky-looking lad there, with the dark eyes and the long black fringe?

For all my bookishness, I just loved soccer. Saturday was easily the best day of the week. Mum would bring me home from having played a game; I'd jump in the bath to bring life back into my half-frozen body and to let whole clumps of mud peel away from my legs. Then, warm again, I'd lie on the couch watching the soccer preview on TV at 1pm, daydreaming that it was me slotting home the long-range volley to the rapturous cries of the crowd and the astonished superlatives of the commentators.

One Saturday morning, and I can't now remember the name of our opponents, the 'C' team were in action again. At half time we had been losing six-nil and the only question was whether our opponents would get to double figures or not. It was a typical 'C' team game, a mismatch; the other side were much bigger and much more surefooted than us. For most of the second half we chased the ball like a starving pack of dirty mongrels after a rat. If, by chance, one of us did get the ball, the rest would be yelling: 'pass, pass, give it to me! Pass it!' All of us, in our daydreams, were stars. To be fair, we were all so starved of the rush that comes with being in possession of the ball that our desire to get the briefest touch of it was understandable.

***

A drizzly grey Saturday morning. The game is being played entirely in our half of the field. No sooner do we kick the ball away than it comes straight back at us. That is, until the moment when Rory hoofs a mighty clearance high in the air, up towards the left wing. There are three people with any chance of getting near the ball as it lands: Deano, who has been living in his own world somewhere in the middle of the field, their defender, and me. I'm left-footed and having been assigned the position of left back had loyally stuck to it, even when I was entirely on my own in that particular muddy patch of the field.

All three of us chase hard and Deano wins. This isn't too surprising, because he is actually quite athletic and does orienteering for Leinster. What is astonishing, however, is what happens next. The ball is descending fast towards him. Since I'm pretty close, he probably should try to head it, or even better, chest it towards me. But everyone on our side knows what would be the result of that. Deano may be fast but he's got no co-ordination. The ball is going to bounce off him and fly away in an almost random direction.

As the ball lands, Deano swivels, sticking out his leg with his foot held up, making an L-shaped cup to catch it in. The momentum of the ball is deadened. Perfectly. It rolls to the side, right in front of me, about two yards away. There is an audible gasp of awe from some of our players, although perhaps that is just in my head. I nearly stop running in surprise. Deano sprints off ahead of me, down the left wing. I look up to see the defender hesitate. Should he cover Deano or come for me and the ball? The problem is, none of his teammates are close; they've all been caught out, pushing up, looking for their own moment of glory, a goal.

With a look of resolution, the defender bursts into action and charges towards me. I boot the ball past him and it's not a bad pass in that at least it doesn't hit the defender or go out of play. Then I tear off towards their goal, while the defender turns to chase the ball and Deano. This is fantastic. We are in the opponent's half, with a real chance of scoring. All their team are streaming back; our own players are standing still, watching, wondering. Is it possible? Can it be that we have played so sweetly for once that it is us bearing down on their goal?

My legs are driving me on, my breath is ragged. I've got to get to the goalmouth. Deano laughs aloud with excitement as he kicks the ball onward and chases it. Their defender can't keep up with him. So it's up to their goalkeeper, who starts to come forward. He must have spent the entire game until now trying to keep warm on his own. He is tentative, crouched. Deano kicks the ball again, to the side of the goalkeeper, away from the goal. He's trying to take it around the keeper, but I wince, it's too close. They both chase the ball towards the left-hand corner flag and Deano gets there first. He hoofs it across towards me with a cry 'Liam!', and then he falls on his back from the twisted shape he had to make to get the ball over to me.

This is the moment: a muddy spinning ball, coming fast, almost, but not quite, going into the goal. It takes one bounce, then another and it's here. I'm here. I'm in front of an open goal, a yard away. No opponents are anywhere near. The goal beckons. I've seen it so often on television: the triumphant moment when the net stretches, receiving the ball. I've done it so often myself, when there was no one else watching, whacked the ball into the goal, to listen to the sighing, rushing, sound it makes as it hits and slides down the white cord netting. But never in a real game, never when the hopes of a team who have not scored a goal in eleven matches are resting on me.

I stick out my foot; the ball hits my knee and flies up over the bar. The goal is still empty, the net flaccid.

I've missed.

The shame is indescribable. It was far, far harder to miss in this situation than to score. If the ball had hit me in the stomach, the face, anywhere, if it had hit my shin, my foot, I would have scored. But somehow I managed to scoop it up and over the bar. I've let everyone down. That goal should have been the culmination of the most beautiful football we had ever played and instead the whole opportunity serves to illustrate more than any scoreline the fact that the 'C' team are the school's donkeys. Losing is expected of us, but for a moment we dreamed of scoring. Look and laugh at the collapse of our hopes. Look at how we had the easiest scoring chance ever to come about in a game of football and we missed it. I honestly didn't care for my own part, well, only a little. What was really stinging and making hot tears come unwanted to my eyes was the feeling that I had ruined everything. My team were all at the point of leaping about, cheering and celebrating, a pent-up eleven games worth of celebration; I could sense it. Now those feelings were to be driven back, a big heavy lid put on them with a slam.

No, it couldn't be. There had to be an alternative.

That's when I first consciously saw them – awareness breaking through the barriers of perception, driven by desperation and shame. There were hundreds, thousands of alternatives. Universes were constantly splitting away from this moment. I picked one nearby and moved into it. It was like holding a balloon in front of your face and squeezing it. I could feel something stretch and I screwed up my eyes, knowing that if it did give way, the rupture would be explosive. There was no sound, but something very serious snapped. Somewhere there was a bang, a meteorite destroying Siberia, the trees all lined up along the ground for hundreds of miles, radiating away from the impact. That's a metaphor by the way; I'm just saying what it felt like and how even then I knew what I had done would have repercussions.

**

The ball was in the net. I'd tapped it in with no difficulty. My new memory confirmed the simple kick. Just like the first time I'd moved, I felt disorientated, having two memories of the same moment. But the old one, the miss, quickly faded, not that it disappeared. It became rather grey and unreal, like a day-dream.

'Yaaay!'

'Goal!'

'Yes!'

'Get in there!'

'Goal!'

The shouting, cheering and general happiness was everything I had anticipated. It really did make the difference. Not only did the team play much better after that but our opponents also showed us respect, at least to the extent of keeping defenders back and marking us. I'm sure that every one of the 'C' team went home happy that afternoon; it didn't matter that we had lost 8:1.

'Mum.'

'Yes dear?'

'I scored a goal today.'

'Did you dear? Well done.'

She was right, the goal wasn't that important. What really mattered was that I'd learned that the ability which had come to me in the barge accident had not gone away. I'd learned how to move.

3

Steering Towards Trouble

That night I lay in bed, looking at the stars, the dayglo ones I had put up in pretty good approximation of real constellations. When you lose a tooth, but before the new one grows through, you have a place in your mouth that your tongue keeps coming back to, until you get used to it. For a while it is raw and ticklish. Well, my whole body was like that. I was that space and I felt uncomfortable, like the universe was licking me, getting used to me.

There was something more.

The closest you can get to visualising infinity is to put two mirrors together and examine the way that the reflections echo back and forth. It's not actually possible to see an infinite number of images though, for two reasons. One is that your own eye gets in the way of a perfect alignment. The other is that each time light bounces off the silver behind the glass a few less photons come back. Eventually, even if you had a light as bright as the sun, the images would become sluggish and peter out in darkness. In reality, in your bedroom say, the best you can do is shine a bright light on two mirrors that are not quite opposite, and then you see long corridors of reflection, sinking into the depths.

That is exactly what I felt as I lay in bed. All around me, in every direction, were other universes. The nearest ones were bright and they were very similar to the one I was in. Here, I had left my socks on the floor; there, my duvet was upside-down. I didn't focus on them all, because I could sense there were millions of them. All around us, all the time, the universe was seething with alternatives. How had I not seen it before? It seemed very natural to me now, to exist in a particular universe whilst being surrounded by all the other ones, millions of echoes.

You remember that when I told my story about the barge accident to Zed, my version was slightly different to his? Well, I realised excitedly, I could now see why. All the universes around me were slightly different. I hadn't moved from the barge to home that time; I'd moved to a different universe where I'd been too sick to go on the school trip. That other universe had been slightly different to my original one in lots of small ways.

With my eyes closed, I tried to see more clearly into the

alternate universes. It was hard work to reach out with my mind for the ones that were further away, but they did exist. I found one in which Mum came up with a glass of water. Since I was thirsty and I wanted to talk to her, I made the effort to go to it. Again, resistance. Trying again, I didn't have shame or desire to help me and I stopped before I felt the rupture open, but then I got a little angry with myself for being frightened. Was I going to give up on something amazing because of some vague feeling that it was wrong? What was I afraid of? This time I tried I gritted my teeth and pushed hard for the universe I wanted; sweat broke out all over my body, but I felt something tear and I fell through.

'Liam.' Mum tapped softly on the door. 'Are you awake? Would you like a drink?'

'Yes please, Mum.'

She put it beside the bed.

'Mum?'

'Yes?'

'Can you move universes?'

'What do you mean?'

'Like, can you see lots of alternative universes, all spread out around you? And can you move to the one you want?'

'No.' She got up to go, a little distant now. I knew she worried about me, wondered if I spent too much time indoors on my own. But this was important, so I tried again.

'It's like you are in a bright light and there are other places beside you, in the shadows, but you can move to them, bringing the light with you. Don't you get that?'

She put her hand on my head.

'You are hot, Liam. Drink your water.'

I drank some.

'No, but, Mum, do you?'

'No, Liam.' She was cold, deliberately discouraging me from this kind of chat. She wanted me to be normal, to talk about normal things, whatever they were. I gave up. In a way it was good that she didn't understand me; the discovery was my own. And I was going to keep it that way. This was my chance to become someone else, someone admired and strong, a hero. I resolved not even to tell Zed any more about it, not until I was ready.

* * *

Once I had got the hang of moving, I did it all the time. Of course I did. I was nearly sixteen and I had discovered an amazing way of solving all life's difficulties. That there was a price to pay for this awesome ability should have been obvious to me. After all, I did have a growing sensation that somewhere I'd awoken a beast with an appetite the size of a planet. It crept into my dreams.

There was a recurrent nightmare I had where I was a wolf and I was starving. But no matter how often I killed and ate, I just couldn't devour enough to keep hunger from driving me on in a frenzy of desperation, even to the point where I ate my own young.

My worries, however, were less important than the fact that I could mess around as never before, because whenever anything went wrong I simply moved to a different universe.

Like when Michael Clarke was in the cupboard.

* * *

It was a boring Thursday lunchtime. Zed was hunched in the little wooden press underneath the blackboard at the top of the class.

'Hey, Liam, close the door a sec.'

A moment later his muffled voice came out.

'It's really dark in here.'

'Let's see.' Deano came over and took a turn. 'Yeah. It really is.'

At this point I looked up and caught Michael Clarke's eye. He was sitting at his desk, doing his homework, like a good boy. He hid his interest in what we were doing with a sneer and looked down quickly, not wanting to draw attention to himself. He was, after all, a little afraid of my friends and certainly of me.

I'd changed a lot since discovering that I could move. In the past, I would have been just like Michael. Now, I was a devil. And the funny thing was that nobody else could see the change, not even my mum, because for them, in this universe, I'd always been a bit of a terror. I liked the fact that my mum no longer worried if I was spending too much time alone on the computer. Instead her main concern was that I was going to get into serious trouble at school. She didn't know that my cockiness was based on my knowing for certain that whatever

I got up it, it would turn out all right.

When I looked back to the cupboard, I winked at my friends, in the hope we could play a trick on Michael.

'You know, most human beings can't tolerate being in a dark confined space for very long. It's called claustrophobia.' My voice was just loud enough that I was certain Michael could hear me. 'Zed, I bet you can't stay in there a minute.'

'A minute? Sure I can.' Zed climbed in and we pushed the door shut. After about thirty seconds, he banged it open. 'Let me out! That's horrible.' When it comes to devilment, Zed is really quick on the uptake. I'd learned it all from him.

'OK, that's thirty-five seconds for Zed.' I was pretending to look at my new digital watch. 'Your turn, Deano.'

By now Deano had got it. He didn't last much longer.

'Forty-four seconds,' I announced and looked around the room. 'Anyone else?'

I'm sure that Tara appreciated the psychology of the situation, because she looked up from her group of friends, disgusted. But as far as Michael was concerned, here were three of the most admired boys in the class, behaving feebly in the face of a challenge that any idiot could succeed in. He stood up, put his pen cap properly back on his pen – he was the first to have a real ink pen – strode over full of confidence and sat in the cupboard.

'Time me.'

'Thirty seconds. Keep going, Michael.'

'A minute! Go, Michael!'

'Two minutes.'

At three minutes, Zed couldn't help letting out a snort of laughter and we heard the faintest of whimpers.

'Oh no.'

'I'm afraid so.'

No sooner had he got inside and pulled the door shut than I had silently lowered the latch, so he couldn't get out. For a while he pleaded with us, but we weren't even listening. We were at the back of the class designing logos for 'Inextreme', the band we intended to form. Then Michael banged on the door for a few minutes, fast at first, becoming more intermittent as he became disheartened.

Towards the end of lunch break, two teachers came into the classroom, the usual dinner patrol to check everything was all right. We went silent and Michael must have sensed the change in atmosphere, because he started kicking the side of the press.

If you ask everyone in my class what happened next, nobody will remember how it first went, which is that the teachers let him out and he blamed me. Locking Michael in a cupboard was pretty harmless really, but my mum and dad were getting fed up with complaints from school. I didn't want them to get another. So even as the teachers were about to get involved, I searched out other paths. No one in this universe remembers the version where I got in trouble because I moved, to a universe in which, just as the teachers entered our classroom and the talking stopped, I began drumming with my ruler on the desk. Zed picked up the beat. Deano thumped the covers of a textbook together for the bass. Lots of my other classmates joined in. It was like a samba band. The teachers could tell something was up, from our grinning faces, but they didn't care enough to investigate and left us to it.

'Close one,' muttered Zed.

'No kidding.' In more than two-thirds of the possible universes they'd heard the noises from the cupboard and released Michael, who vented his annoyance by getting me into trouble.

Before long, in twos and threes, the rest of our class returned and we were all sitting in proper silence when Miss Nolan came back in from lunch. After she had sat down and opened a textbook, she took a steady look around the class. It wasn't long before she noticed Michael's empty desk.

'Where is Michael Clarke? He was here this morning.'

There was this tense feeling in the room. Most of us knew he was in the cupboard. He must have felt the attention of thirty eyes on the door of his dark prison. But he didn't make a sound. Strangely, even though it clearly wasn't his fault as he was locked in from the outside, he was so terrified of getting into trouble with Miss Nolan that he didn't bang on the door or anything. Presumably he was now hoping to wait it out; that we'd let him out after the class was over.

'Does anyone know where Michael Clarke is?' asked Miss Nolan.

Zed put up his hand and I looked at him curiously. What was he going to say? Was he going to make up an outrageous story?

'Yes, Zimraan?'

'He's in the cupboard, miss.'

I couldn't help but start sniggering at the brazen cheek of my comrade. There were a few other giggles too and those who didn't know what had happened in the lunch break now looked up with amazement.

Miss Nolan turned around slowly to stare at the cupboard. Poor Michael, what was he thinking? My sniggering got worse and it set Deano off. The more we tried to fight it, the more the tears came.

'Michael Clarke, are you in there?'

Silence, a palpable, fecund, wonderful silence. All eyes were focused on that little cupboard in which Michael was suffering. We were chortling aloud now, at the back of the class, and that was getting the others going. Part of the emotion fuelling our giggles was extreme nervousness. Miss Nolan would see that he'd been locked in from the outside and she could very easily turn on us, the perpetrators.

With a heavy sigh she got up, unlatched the door and pulled it wide open.

Michael didn't dare look at her but put his legs out first, and then struggled up onto his feet, head bowed. She regarded him with dismay, before shaking her head.

'Go back to your desk.'

It was impossible to contain ourselves any longer and the laughter rang out until exhausted and gasping for breath, we laid our heads on our desks, spent. Tara was furious with us, I know. And of course, with hindsight, I'm not proud of creating such a painful moment for Michael. Mind you, it was funny: the whole class looking at that silent cupboard where we knew Michael was trying his hardest to disappear.

Anyway, there are a hundred stories like that one. The point is I could get away with anything. You can see as well, that my new powers didn't make me a better person. More confident, bold, reckless even, yes, but kind? Unfortunately not.

***

Rather more serious was my campaign against Mr Kenny. At least that was justifiable. What I didn't like about Mr Kenny was the way he made fun of us at swimming. I get angry even now, when I remember how he would humiliate the boys. He would shout at us across the pool.

'When are you going to get hairs on your chest, Liam O'Dwyer? Don't you know you are descended from apes?'

I never really got the point of that remark, though he thought it was clever enough to keep bellowing it out, pretty much every week. The girls were pathetic. They would go along with him, laughing nervously each time he shouted. We were fifteen or sixteen then and even for me, who could move, there were moments of introspection, doubt and uncertainty. When I was in my swimming shorts I felt vulnerable. Anyone would squirm at such an open, public, half-reference to puberty. Mr Kenny knew it too. That's why he kept it up.

Another cause of our dislike of him was his English class. These days I don't mind reading the famous works of literature; they are generally pretty good. But I refuse to look again at *Romeo and Juliet* or *The Lord of the Flies*. I'd never be able to get Mr Kenny's dramatic reading voice out of my head, with its emphases on all the wrong words.

Worse still was his entirely inappropriate crush on Jane Curtis. There was this after-school, drama-class routine. I should have realised sooner, given that the stupid play we worked on, but never performed to anyone, was about two cynical teachers and their suppressed desire for a beautiful pupil. He was cultivating Jane, who was flattered at first but then told me she thought his attentions were going too far, ringing her at home, for example. It all adds up and, while I know Tara disapproves and I probably have taken on a lot of bad karma, I'm glad I got to him in the end. It helped that he had jowls like those of a dog, which he rather pitifully tried to hide under a beard.

With the backup of the boys, I tortured Mr Kenny by barking down the corridor at him, and then running away, before he could see who was doing it. If I hadn't been able to move, he would have caught me a hundred times. Each time he did see me, I just moved to a nearby universe where he hadn't quite been quick enough. As a result, we were in a universe where he'd been driven crazy by my antics.

If I saw him on the stairs: woof, woof! Entering the staff room: woof, woof! Crossing the courtyard: woof, woof! Then I'd drop down below the window. Some weeks he would ignore it; other weeks he would roar with anger and run full pelt for the corner, only to see my heels as I shot out of sight down the far end of a corridor.

For his birthday I left a present on his desk. His chest stuck out with pleasure when he saw the colourful 'Happy Birthday' wrapping. I almost regretted what I had done; he was so touched that his class had gone to the trouble of demonstrating their affections. When he tore away the paper to find a can of dog food, Zed and I sniggered. To his credit, Mr Kenny took the joke relatively well. Those jowls only wobbled a bit in dismay as he attempted a smile.

After a while, it seemed like the whole school was in on the barking. The headmaster even spoke about it at assembly and said that if anyone was caught making barking sounds in the school they would be in very serious trouble. That calmed things down for most, but not for me. I just kept on barking at him. Shrill little barks, big deep woofs. Whatever mood I was in, I'd let him have it with relish, remembering his own humiliating shouts at the swimming pool.

They never caught me. Well, in some universes they did, but those are inhabited by other versions of me. I moved to this one, the one where I finally let him see me, fair and square, near the end of term at the top of the stairs.

'Woof!' I barked angrily, arms folded.

'Aha, Liam O'Dwyer, I knew it was you! I have you at last.'

He ran up the stairs and followed me into the classroom, where I had taken my seat at the back.

'Liam O'Dwyer, you know what the headmaster said about barking in school. I look forward to hearing what your father says when he learns of the trouble you are in.'

'Sir, take me to the headmaster right now. Cane my hand if you like, but please, don't bring my father into it. You don't know what he's like.'

'Liam O'Dwyer, you have been behind the worst breach of

discipline, the most sustained campaign of miscreancy I have ever known in all my time as a teacher. Of course your father must be informed.'

'Sir, no. Please, you don't understand. He'll kill me.' My voice trembled. 'Please, sir. Have a heart.'

'My mind is made up.' Mr Kenny slapped his books down firmly on the desk. 'There is no excuse for your behaviour this term. I shall ring your father this very evening.'

'Is there nothing I can say to make you change your mind?'

'Nothing.'

He sat down and with a very serious expression began to leaf through *The Lord of the Flies*. 'Now turn to page eighty-four.'

I got up, climbed up onto the window ledge and lowered the top window. It squeaked and everyone looked at me.

'Liam O'Dwyer, get down from there at once!'

'I'm sorry, but my life is worth nothing once my father hears from you.'

Our classroom was on the second floor; the drop was a fatal one.

'Get down.' His voice was deliberately tired. 'You are a second-rate actor and you don't fool anyone.'

He was right. But still.

'I'm sorry you don't believe me.' And I jumped out, arms flailing extravagantly.

'Arrrrgh, Nooo!' Mr Kenny leapt up. I could hear the clatter of his desk, flung to the side as he raced across the room and the further crashing of his frantic progress through the class. Then he was above me, staring down from the window, wide-eyed. I looked back up at him and smiled, before straightening up.

There was a small window ledge, which I had been crouched on. It was a bit risky to throw myself out so dramatically, but I reckoned that if something had gone wrong, in the second or two it took me to fall, I could move to a universe where I didn't crash into the playground paving.

'You boy,' he stood, white, trembling all over, 'are a disturbed child and a menace.'

As I climbed back in, Zed gave me the thumbs-up.

'Deadly, Liam. The best ever, really.'

That night Mr Kenny rang my dad for a long chat, but we were ready. For someone from an Asian family background, Zed can do an amazingly convincing impersonation of my dad, northside Dublin accent and all. He and I were sitting there playing *Gran Turismo*, the volume down of course. Zed had the phone cradled on his shoulder. Every now and again he would say, 'terrible sorry, Mr Kenny, terrible sorry,' or, 'the little f..., the little eejit.' Zed finished it off by sounding really angry, 'Ja-ysus! You can be sure that won't be happening again. Wait till I see the little ... Well. You can be sure.'

After that window incident, Mr Kenny never again shouted at me during swimming; he really did think I was a little mad.

4
Girls

I am getting around to Tara. But first, reluctantly, I had better say something about girls. Naturally, being a sixteen-year-old boy I had a great desire for girls, but unusually for that age, because I could move, I also had a lot of scores. I'll spare you the details since they are sleazy, I'll admit, but chasing girls did teach me something about other people's behaviour and moving.

When I search for other options to a physical event, or an event involving me, that's easy. At every moment there are thousands of alternatives, far too many for me to comprehend them all before they fall away, time moving onwards. But the number of options that involve other people changing their actions is much narrower. I can't move to a universe where anything goes. People behave in a manner that is more or less true to their character across all the universes.

What I discovered, though, was that our friends' characters were not always what they seemed. For example, there was a girl in our class called Hazel Cartwright. She was very proper, very aloof. She did ballet after school and scorned the rough side of the class. There was no way she would show the slightest interest in me. Except that, during one very dull geography lesson, I started to daydream and explore some of the more unusual alternate universes. Once I had started to look in all seriousness, I was amazed at the options involving her. There was one where all I had to do was come up to her during a lunch break when we were the only people in the classroom. In my hand I held the key to the storeroom at the back of 4D.

'What's that?' she asked.

I told her.

'Why are you showing me?'

'Come with me now, and we'll have thirty minutes together, in the dark.'

She said nothing more, but followed.

Then there was Jocelyn Doonan who all the boys fancied, some of the girls too. She was cool about it, not showy, just natural, and modest. She had wonderful black curly hair that she would hold to the side when she leant over her desk. Most of the time she wasn't interested in me, although for a while it was all I did, search around fruitlessly for universes in which I got together with Jocelyn.

There was a big dance for Debbie Healy's birthday at the community hall in Tolka Park. Tara wasn't there, but all the trendier people in the class were. For some really strange reason, Jocelyn was in a totally wild humour. I don't know what had happened to her, but when I sought among the nearby universes there were an amazing number of them in which Jocelyn was with me. Then I realised there were even more that didn't concern me, but where she was with another boy. In fact, it would have been possible for every one of the boys in the hall that night, without exception, to score Jocelyn. It was during the slow songs I could see that most clearly. All the adjacent universes showed her with a variety of boys. If they'd started kissing her, had steered her towards a dark corner, she'd have stayed with them.

At the time I was delighted that I could see this before any of my rivals. But, looking back, I feel a little sad. Whatever it was that put her in such a mood was not good. My ability to move is very limited in some ways. But if I had searched, I might have found a universe where she talked to me about what had happened. I feel all protective thinking about it now, when it's too late. I can't move to universes that have branched away from turning points that are far back in time; in fact, a few minutes is my limit.

Sixteen-year-old boys are quick to boast to each other about their conquests. A lot of it is just desperation, not to be left behind, not to be thought a failure at something far more important than exams or sports. With me, though, I didn't boast at all. I never said anything about any girl, until now, writing this down. It would be good to say this was because of my respect for the girls that I was with, but since I'm being honest, science demanding such honesty, I'll admit my discretion came about because I very quickly learned something by watching the consequences of bragging.

Even if you only tell your best mate, the word gets around and girls simply will not go with you. That's how it was for Zed. If he wanted to score, he had to go to events involving girls from St Theresa's, because our girls had closed ranks against him. Girls don't want to get together with someone who is going to boast about it, not just because they don't want to be a conquest, but because they want to enjoy themselves discreetly, without ending up with a reputation.

***

After a while, I began to notice Tara. Despite that terrible day on the barge, it was easy to overlook Tara. After all, she was very quiet. As I've already said, around that time I had been given to speculating on different girls, testing the possibilities. One day I concentrated on her. I had become tired of the 'beautiful' girls, the ones who spent hours upon hours concerned with their looks. The strange thing is, with the possible exception of Jocelyn, the more beautiful the girl, the more obsessed she was that she could have higher cheekbones, or more voluptuous lips, or something along those lines. I saw the other boys feverishly chasing such narcissistic girls and I was slightly contemptuous of them.

One slow school afternoon, I was examining the girls in the class with this new perspective and I thought of Tara. Tara keeps her hair long, in most universes anyway. As it is red, watching her you sometimes get caught in breathtaking moments where you want to be an artist and put her in a painting. Simple moments, like when her hair gathers at the shoulder, then cascades as she leans over to adjust the straps on her false foot, or when she smiles. She doesn't smile often enough.

What about the fact she had only one foot? Of course, you say, what difference does it make? Today I'd agree with you. It makes none. You get so used to her limp; you'd miss it if it were gone. To some extent, it's part of her character now. Back then, though, the lads were ashamed to fancy Tara and, if you said that you did, you'd get a slagging for being creepy, like you had a fetish. Not that I cared about their slagging. I was a lot older than them when it came to girls.

In any case, while I was scrutinising her pattern of possible behaviours, I discovered a really extraordinary quality in Tara, which was that it was very difficult to find a universe where she did a mean or selfish act. Universe upon universe, in their tens of thousands, branching away to infinity, and in nearly all the ones I looked into, they carried her onwards, a genuinely kind and caring human being. Can you see why I was impressed? What had begun as a rather flirtatious daydreaming suddenly became a fascinating and serious challenge.

One dinnertime I went up to her and asked her out.

'Liam O'Dwyer, I think you are selfish, arrogant, cruel and vain. I wouldn't go out with you in a million years.'

That didn't work, so I moved to one where I hadn't left my table and been turned down. Of course I looked around for a universe where she had answered, 'Why, Liam, I'd be delighted.' But it didn't exist. In fact, I got the same answer everywhere, with minor variations: lazy, uncaring, heartless. The best I could do was find a universe in which a fire alarm went off just after I'd spoken to her, so that I couldn't hear her reply. This was frustrating, but it was also interesting: a challenge.

Watching Tara having to stay in the classroom on Wednesday afternoons when we go for P.E. was usually a slightly sad moment, because it reminded everyone of the accident. One Wednesday, I arranged to be excused from P.E. and spent the time with her. I was on my best behaviour, displaying my sensitive side and thought we got on fairly well. So the next day I asked her out again.

'Liam O'Dwyer, I think you are selfish, arrogant, cruel, vain,' she paused for a moment, 'and manipulative. I wouldn't go out with you in a million years.'

Busted. This wasn't going to be easy.

Over the weekend I contemplated various schemes to get her interested in me: fires in which I would be her rescuer; swimming accidents, ditto. It was pathetic really, so I gave up. But I kept my attention on her and the more I saw her steady, true, path through time, the more I knew I wanted to go out with her. What had begun as a challenge was becoming something powerful and out of my control.

It really is hard to explain, but she is almost unique among all the people I know. For example, one hot afternoon in class, her desk was falling shut, just as she noticed a fly landing on the rim. To save the fly, she had to put her hand out, scaring it away and getting a painful blow on her knuckles. It was a tiny thing, but I had to laugh. She literally would not hurt a fly, not in any of the hundreds of nearby universes in which the same incident took place. Similarly, I'd listen in to her conversations, and then search nearby universes for a spiteful comment or a jealous one. Never. No one else stands up to such scrutiny, especially me.

I haven't really commented on this, so while I'm at it, I should point out that being able to see into different universes has a down side. I've seen Zed betray me, Deano blame me for something he knew I didn't do, and much worse. Everyone has their weaknesses. At first I found this distressing. It makes you feel hurt and lonely, but after a while you get used to it. It is a very profound truth that you are on your own in this life and, much as other people might care for you at times, no one consistently looks after your interests. Why should they, when they often let themselves down? I learned to judge my friends not by what they got up to in the more remote universes, but on the overall pattern, on the percentages. In the vast majority of universes Zed is loyal and Deano is honest, so they are my friends. On this scale, a metaversal one, Tara stands out as the best of us all, by a long way.

Naturally, I became curious about how it was she held to her path so consistently, when the rest of us, to various degrees, had our bad moments. In part, it is just something she was born with, I suppose. Then having to catch up with us all, after the accident, to get to a stage where we stopped pitying her and forgot about her foot, that must have been really difficult, and it must have made her tough.

One morning, though, I overheard her talking about Buddhism with surprising enthusiasm, and then things fell into place. She believed that she should be trying to improve herself, all of humanity, and, indeed, all of creation. She believed life for people could be made better and that how she behaved actually made a difference.

It was a revelation; it was humbling. Up until this time of my life, I hadn't ever stopped to think about what I believed in, and it came as a surprise to me that some people had not only thought about what they were going to do with their lives but were living them accordingly. In Tara's case, she ascribed to some quite sophisticated ideas, which amounted to striving to be a better person by making a positive contribution to the world.

This really set me thinking, because with my ability, perhaps the world could be made a better place. Up to this time, it suddenly dawned on me with a flush of shame, I had used my discovery entirely for myself. But I could just as easily use it for everyone.

Next time Deano found himself struggling in French and the butt of Mr Brown's dry sarcasm, I moved, to an admittedly rare universe where he had actually done his homework and came out of the interrogation admirably and with praise. Deano basked; I basked.

Then I really tried to do some good, some serious good. My dad works as a fitter at the Mater Hospital. In the hope of being able to save lives, I went to the Accident and Emergency Department there. That plan turned out to be very boring and a little sad. The problem was that I couldn't make much of a difference by the time someone came in. Seeing the lack of options for the chronically sick people was depressing. Thousands of universes and they were suffering in them all. Where I was needed was at the scene of accidents, where the options for choosing a new universe were still available. It made me think that I should become a firefighter or an ambulance driver.

If you think about it carefully, what I was trying to do doesn't make a great deal of sense. Just because I could move to a universe where someone survived an accident didn't save them in the universe I'd left behind, or all the other ones like it. But back then I wasn't so clear of what my ability involved. In any case, I'm still rather proud of the moment. It was the first time I began to think of others and not just myself.

Not that this flash of moral behaviour led me to reappraise the whole moving thing. It was second nature to me by then. Even though I was filled with a sensation that something very fearsome and menacing was growing in power, I couldn't stop moving. Could anyone give up an ability like that?

***

Trying to be a good person didn't mean I made quick progress with Tara. It took nearly a year from my change in attitude before she would let me into her life. The breakthrough came about halfway through fifth year, during one lunch break when I came and sat beside her.

'I know how to improve the karma of the people around me.'

Tara was interested in that, but sceptical. 'How?'

'Well, you have to be willing to believe something pretty strange.'

'Go on.'

'Imagine, for a moment, that you can swap into nearby universes.'

'Nearby universes?'

'Yeah. Exactly like this one, but with small differences. This eraser is blue instead of red. Sheila walks through that door now, instead of later.'

'Right. So?'

'So,' I paused, 'you keep moving all the time, to a better universe. Each time someone nearby makes a choice, you can move to the universe where they were kind, or considerate, or helpful.' She was listening carefully, for the first time ever we were having a proper conversation. 'It might take a million moves, but eventually you would be in a universe where people had only ever done good deeds. Then you would be close to nirvana, right? Not just for yourself, but for everyone?'

'Maybe. Although I think nirvana is a place you reach after you have left all cares behind. It's not really a question of making the right choices within this world.'

'But it would be close right? It would be like living in a world full of true Buddhists.' I could see Tara was taking me seriously. She studied the eraser in my hand and then wondered aloud, 'A world where all the people had only ever done positive actions? It would still be part of samsara, the cycle of life and death. But more people would be at a level that would allow them to escape. That would be good.'

We sat for a moment, in shared contemplation. We were talking about something important, and I really liked the feeling. Then she looked up with a frown. 'When I move universes, what happens to the one I leave behind, the one where they made a bad choice?'

Ahh, sharp. Way ahead of me, who could actually move. 'They are still there. It's just that you are no longer experiencing them.'

'Well then, you've not really solved anything. In fact, a true Buddhist would probably stay in the darker world and learn how to let go of suffering rather than escape to a happy Teletubby land.'

For a moment my gaze met her shining grey eyes and I felt lightning crawl around the inside of my head. This was a whole new perspective on my life and my ability.

'I need to talk about this,' I stated earnestly. 'I have to think about these things, they are important.' With one sentence she had made me reconsider the entire direction of my life. What was I going to do with my skill? She began to laugh, that I was taking what to her must have seemed idle conversation so seriously, but then she looked at my face and, after a moment's hesitation, she gave a small nod.

'We can talk about it in Café Paradiso after school, if you like.'

5

A Cruel Valentine

That Wednesday, after P.E., I hurried down to Café Paradiso, to find Tara waiting for me, a glass of orange juice on the table in front of her. She smiled when she saw me come in. The café was already filling up with kids from our fifth and sixth years. Meeting Tara here wasn't a big deal, like a date. This is where a lot of us hung out after school. But still, here she was, waiting for me. And she looked pleased that I'd arrived.

'What are you reading?' I asked her, throwing down my bag. Tara had put her book face down on the table and I picked it up. *The Handmaid's Tale*. The spine was broken in several places and I ran my finger over the ridges.

'You know there are two types of people in this world,' I spoke solemnly as I settled into an uncomfortable metal chair, 'those who treat their books well and the other kind, the brutal kind. You can tell a lot about someone by how they treat their books.'

'Yeah? Show me one of yours.'

I didn't usually bring books in to school, so I moved in order to get one. Curiously, the book that I was most likely to bring with me was *The Catcher in the Rye*. This said more about the fact that I wanted to make a good impression than my true reading interests, which were usually biographies about footballers or science fiction. Taking it from me, Tara was genuinely amazed at how unmarked it was.

'Have you started reading this? It's like new.'

'Finished it.' Which was true in this universe. I'd rather liked it. It made me wish I had a little sister.

'No way.' She laughed again. 'You are right, you can tell a lot about someone by their books. In your case, beneath your disguise as a troubled hooligan, you are really a repressed nerdy type.'

Her grey eyes were sparkling and I was smiling happily back at her.

'You know, I really can move universes.' It just came right out. I hadn't planned on telling her, but then again, I was getting lonely, being able to move but not sharing it with anyone. I had been thinking of a way I could explain it to Zed and I guess that led me to just blurt it out, like a fool.

Tara's expression instantly changed to one of mistrust, perhaps anticipating an attempt by me to mock her. She looked down and seemed to need to adjust the straps on her leg.

'I'm not making it up. I can prove it.'

'Really?' She frowned.

'Easily. Write down a number between one and twenty.'

She got out a pen and was about to write in the back of her book.

'Wait, use this.' I gave her my school rough book. I couldn't bear to see her mark a real book.

Before Tara put away *The Handmaid's Tale*, she folded down the corner of a page to mark her place. My involuntary wince caused the hint of a smile to weaken the sternness of her expression.

'Look.' I produced a bookmark, put it in the right place and unfolded the page corner. 'These were invented for a reason.'

'Thanks.' Her pen was poised over the page of my rough book. 'All right, turn away.'

I gave her a moment to write down her number.

'Seventeen,' I announced. 'Write down another.'

Her eyebrows rose a little.

'Four. Write down another.'

This time she looked over her shoulder, checking if there was a reflection or some other means by which I could see the number. Before setting down the next one, she hunched up over the book, shielding it with her hand and a cascade of red hair.

'Twelve.'

There was a curious interplay of emotions on her face. Doubt was giving way to puzzlement and, thankfully, amazement. She was not rejecting me but was growing curious, entering into my world. We filled a page of the book with numbers, before I stopped the game. I was tired of moving now and a pain was growing in my mind that was manageable until I came at it the wrong way, when it stabbed me in the side of my head.

'How are you doing that?' she whispered, leaning forward in complicity.

'I can see hundreds, thousands even, of nearby universes. I've been moving to the ones where I guessed right.'

'So all those philosophical questions of yours, they were not hypothetical?'

'No.'

'You could really find a universe where people have only ever been kind to each other?'

'Well, I could keep moving in that direction. I'm not sure if I'd ever reach it though.'

'Why don't you do it?'

'I might. But I kinda like it around here.'

***

It was such a relief to have someone to confide in, that for the next few days I was walking around with bright enthusiasm for life. Hail and cold rain may have been assailing the windows of our classrooms, but summer had come to my heart. Yet this glorious happiness lasted no more than two weeks, ending with the arrival of Valentine's Day.

The previous year I had moved to a universe where I had, anonymously, sent everyone in my class a Valentine's Day card.

I thought it would cheer everyone up. Hopefully it did. But this year to do the same would have felt disloyal to Tara. We were getting on well now, meeting once a week after school. Our growing intimacy had not escaped the notice of Zed and Deano, but they didn't slag me about it. Perhaps they had recognised how serious I was about her; that Tara was not a subject for teasing. Perhaps also we were all getting a bit older.

The first sign something was wrong was the way that Jocelyn Doonan walked past me in the corridor outside our class, face white with fury.

'How could you?' she hissed as she marched past.

Odd. Jocelyn and I got on fairly well.

On opening the door to our classroom, things got even stranger. The whole room went quiet. Tara rushed out past me, her gait awkward, face down. Two of her best friends hurried after her.

'What's up?' I asked Debbie, but she just turned away. So did everyone else. They were all leaving the class, on account of the fact that I had come in. It was slightly frightening, like being in a zombie film or something, but I held my nerve and went over to my desk, giving Deano a rueful shake of my head, showing him that I thought the situation was crazy.

'Not cool, Liam. Not cool.' Deano stood up and joined those walking out of the classroom.

Just a few minutes had passed since I had entered the room. Only Zed was left, and even he was looking at the door, as if making up his mind to go.

'What is it I'm supposed to have done, Zed?' My heart was

racing, as far as I knew nobody in our school had ever been given this treatment; it had to be serious.

'Aww, man.' Zed handed me a Valentine card. The envelope simply had 'Tara' written on it. Inside there was a card that looked like it had come from a gift shop, all shiny and colourful. On the outside was a cute looking cherub. The headline was 'You are my angel!' Inside it read 'Awkward, Nightmarish, Grotesque, Elephantine, Lopsided!' The accompanying cartoon was of a one-legged girl jumping across the card from left to right, with a voice in a bubble shouting 'Hop off!'

Fire and rage seethed through me.

'Who dared make this card? I'll find them and kill them! How could they?' It didn't take much imagination to picture Tara opening the card, probably with some pleasure and excitement, only to be crushed by the message and the evidence that someone held a savage hatred towards her. Never since her accident, and probably never before then either, would anyone have taunted her in such a vicious and cruel manner.

Zed was studying me carefully. 'Look at the handwriting.'

I did. It was a very good forgery; the lettering looked exactly like my own.

'I see. It looks like mine, but I never sent it. Jaysus, Zed, how could I?'

'I dunno, mate.' With a loud sigh, Zed sat in Deano's seat, which was next to mine at the back of the class. 'But Jocelyn says she saw you put this in Tara's desk early this morning, before anyone was in.'

'No way. Why would she say that?' Really, that was the

question. Why on earth would Jocelyn make that up? I was totally bemused. With my head in my hands, eyes closed, I began to search the adjacent universes. Up until now, I had been upset, but not worried. If situations became crappy, and they didn't get much more crappy than this, I could always use my ability and bail. Sod them all, if they thought so little of me. How easily they believed that I could do that to Tara.

Disconcertingly, though, there was no way around this catastrophe. As far as I could see, thousands of distant, dim universes away, there was the hated card. In many universes I was totally alone in the classroom, not even Zed was present. Ever since I had learned to move I had been able to escape difficult situations. Not this one. It was a terrible surprise and, at the same time, a little frightening, to have lost my control over the options available to me.

There was something wrong about the card itself. It was glittering black and evil in all adjacent universes, twisting them, drawing them around it, not letting me see any universe in which it did not exist. It was like the card itself was fighting me. Up until this moment, my fears about the consequences of moving had only been forebodings. Now, however, they were made tangible by this creepy card. What was even more frightening was my sense that this was only the beginning of even worse troubles.

'Zed, you have to believe me. Somehow I've been framed.' My voice was surprisingly even and I kept the tears back.

'Are you callin' Jocelyn a liar? She doesn't seem like the type.'

'No. She's not a liar.'

He sighed, a long heavy sigh. 'Maybe you were there, but put another card in. Some jealous guy swapped it on you.'

Nice one, Zed, to offer me a way out.

'Thanks, mate, but nope. I made her a card, but it's still in my bag.'

'Show me.'

Opening my bag, I got a sinking feeling. There was no card, not even when I had tipped everything out on to the desk.

'Dude.' Zed got up in disgust and left me alone in the classroom.

When, eventually, everyone had to come back in for registration, no one spoke to me; they hardly even exchanged a word with each other. There was a very conspicuous space in the middle of the class: Tara's empty desk.

Enforced solitude gave me a lot of time to think. Firstly, I was bitter with my entire class. If they thought me capable of sending such a card, then I was better off without them. I'd always felt myself to be a little apart, what with being able to move, so this unjustified hostility now created a massive crevasse between us where there had previously just been a crack. I was an island, or better still, a planet, with the vast black silence of space between me and any other life or colour.

Secondly, I wanted vengeance on whoever had done this. They had hurt me and they had hurt the best person I knew, the one person whom I knew was trustworthy, the one person who knew my secret. For two weeks I'd been happy. I had felt that I was not alone. But of course I was. Everyone was. Me most of all.

***

That night I had an alarming dream.

***

I was a demon in the realms beneath the universe and I was hungry. My whole body ached with insatiable desires. My appetite was not for food but for emotion: for guilt, pride, vengeance, anger and fear. A thousand years passed: a thousand years of constant motion, searching through the darkness for the heady emotions of human existence. Perhaps it was millions of years. They seemed to pass all at once, yet existence was a constant agony of unfulfilled desire. At last, I felt my time had come. Somewhere, there was a fraying of the fabric that separated the demon realms and the human universe. A tear, a wound, and I could smell food beyond it. I sniffed, circled, worried at it, feeling it widen, deepen, feeling the pressure build up against it. Finally, it was wide enough and, with an explosion of dark matter, I was through. Gods in the heavens tremble! For I was trapped no longer and could feast until my belly burst or there was nothing more on this earth for me to devour.

***

The first thing I did when I woke up was phone Tara. Surprisingly, her mother answered.

'Who is it?'

'Liam O'Dwyer.'

'Don't ring this number again.' She hung up.

So I sent a text.

'Tara. It wasn't me. U no my secret. Sometin is goin wrong. I need 2 speak 2 u. Help me.'

After a short delay I got a text back.

'OK whr + whn?'

Thank heavens. At last. A chance to turn this miserable situation around.

6
Buddhism and Biscuits

Not only did Tara start talking to me again, but after she'd seen how troubled I was by the hurtful Valentine's Day card and the way it had forced its way into all the possible universes around us, she offered to take me to someone who she thought might be able to help me understand my ability and my fears.

Over the course of the previous year, Tara had been going to the Buddhist centre in Inchicore, where she'd become friends with one of the disciples, an elderly man called Geoffrey Halpin. Tara had got on so well with Geoffrey that they'd reached a point where she would sometimes ring him and call over to visit.

Master Halpin lived in old Kilmainham, in a red-brick cottage. I thought that Tara called him 'master', because he was a martial arts expert or something, but I found out later that it was just that Geoffrey believed that if women had to change from 'Miss' to 'Mrs' when they got married, men ought to have a similar distinction. So he was 'master', as opposed to 'mister', to indicate that he was unmarried.

Tara met me in town and we got the number 19 together. Sitting upstairs, side-by-side on the narrow seat, I was conscious of the softness of her skin when her bare arm brushed mine and I welcomed the fact that our bus was swaying, bringing us inadvertently together.

'Do it again.'

'All right. Pick a number.' I glanced at her and she nodded.

'Forty-seven.'

'Amazing. Do it again.'

This time I couldn't find a universe in which I had the right answer.

'You haven't picked a number.'

'Yes I have.'

I concentrated, pushing hard.

'Jaysus, Tara. You've just created thousands of other universes where I make a fool of myself. Twelve thousand, seven hundred and twenty-two.'

'Of all people, Liam O'Dwyer, I can't believe it's you who can do this.'

'Why not?'

'Because it is a gift. And you are such a messer.'

'Am I?'

'Look at the way you treat Michael. Or Mr Kenny.'

'Yeah. Well, Dog Face. He deserves all he gets.'

'Oh stop. Or I'll start to think you really did send that card.'

We bounced along for a while in silence. She had withdrawn slightly and I no longer felt the warmth of her arm against mine when the bus leaned.

'Who is your favourite author?' I asked her.

'Doris Lessing.'

'I've read one of her books.'

'Really? I wouldn't have thought you'd like her.'

'She wrote a science-fiction book, right? Where this person is on a planet trying to help people get to heaven? And it turns out to be Earth. I liked the start, before it got to modern times. That was a bit boring then.'

'She wrote a few science-fiction books, if you can call them that. The whole point of them is that it makes you see our world through new eyes.'

'Yeah, well. That kind of thing doesn't work for me any more, not now I can see all the other universes.' I paused. 'Do you think Master Halpin really can help me find out what's going on?'

She shrugged, perhaps a little offended by my scepticism.

'He might. At least he will help you think about it in the right way.'

The bus emptied when it reached Rialto. As the woman in front of us got up to leave she turned around and gave a book to Tara.

'I've finished with this. Here, you have it.'

'Oh, thank you. That's only just out.' Tara looked at the cover admiringly, holding the book with both her hands. *Spies I Have Known and Other Stories* by Doris Lessing.

Then she shook back her hair so that that she could look at me clearly, eyes wide with astonishment. Although inside I was totally wrecked from the effort of finding this universe, I tried to smile back and display a casual nonchalance.

'You know, there has to be something wrong with this. There has to be a cost.' Tara had noticed, perhaps, that I was sweating all over.

'Why?'

'I don't know. It just doesn't seem right that you get something for nothing.'

I worried about this too. It was true that there was a cost. Not just the physical effort of moving to remote universes, but there was more. Somewhere in the darkness out beyond the universes I could sense there was a feral animal, sniffing around eagerly. Each time I moved, I was tearing through fabric between universes that shouldn't be damaged. Was the beast getting stronger? Was I making a trail for it? Why was it I had not been able to escape from the bitter experience brought about by that card?

***

A white-haired man answered the door of the red-brick cottage and the many lines of his face immediately formed into a sincere smile when he saw Tara. There was nothing unusual about him at all. He was dressed in jeans and a jumper, like a million other Dubliners.

'Master Halpin, this is Liam O'Dwyer.'

'Call me Geoffrey.' His grip was firm. 'Come inside.'

What would you expect if you visited the house of a Buddhist? I didn't have a clue, but I had been anticipating something unusual, big tapestries on the walls, or no seats, only bare floors. Maybe that it would be filled with the scent of burning incense. But the cottage was exactly like any other place, with chairs and tables, even a TV. The only difference from our house, say, was that on the mantelpiece was a little brass Buddha, sitting in the famous lotus position. On the wall was a framed picture of a bald man in a maroon robe. He was smiling and looking out at the room through very unfashionable large round glasses.

'That's the Dalai Lama.' Geoffrey noticed my gaze.

'Friendly lookin' fella.'

Beside me, Tara stiffened, sensing a note of disrespect in my voice, but I was just thinking of something to say.

'Yes, he's a very warm person.'

'Did you ever meet him?' Tara asked Geoffrey.

'Several times. He made a very strong impression on me, a very calm, dignified man.'

Geoffrey gestured at me to sit at the table.

'Tea?'

'Sure.'

'It's just green tea, I'm afraid.'

'That's fine,' I replied, but I'd never heard of green tea. Tea was brown in my experience.

Tara and I said nothing while we waited. She was anxious

perhaps, although whether it was on my behalf or his I had no idea. Looking along the bookshelves, I saw there were lots of books about religion and Buddhism as you might expect, but there were also some other surprising titles, like a whole set of Calvin and Hobbes cartoons.

Soon Geoffrey was back. On the tray he carried was a pot of tea, three mugs and a plate with some chocolate digestives. A bit decadent for a Buddhist, I thought, but I didn't really know why I felt that Buddhists shouldn't eat chocolate biscuits.

'Tara says you have some interesting spiritual questions.'

'I have.' I paused. 'Did she tell you I can change universes?'

'She did, but I would like to hear your account.'

'Well, it's like this. Right now the universe is dividing up in all directions. I can see one where you are spilling the tea, another where Tara is smiling at something you said – lots and lots of alternatives. If I want, and the universe is not too far away, I can swap into it.'

'I see.' Geoffrey looked carefully at me.

'I can prove it.'

'Can you now?'

'Yes. Think of a number between one and a hundred.'

'Go on.'

'Forty-two.'

'Interesting, you just moved into the universe in which your guess was correct?'

'Yes.'

'What about the universes where you got it wrong?'

I had a quick look around, before they faded.

'They are branching away, disappearing for me. Hey though,' I paused to glance at him, 'even where I guessed wrong, in some of them you are willing to believe me.'

'But this is the universe in which I am most convinced?'

'I think so.'

'Well, it's true. I think that I would be sympathetic to your statement in most universes.' He got up and ran his finger across the back of a number of books before stopping and pulling out a slender volume. 'According to many accounts of the life of Buddha, he existed, and to some extent still exists, in millions of worlds. This book says, for example, that after he achieved enlightenment, and I quote: He emanated into all the human realms of the thousand million cosmic systems with which he was associated.'

I was excited by the description. It was very like the way the universe felt to me. It was not, in fact, one universe but a thousand million cosmic systems – a metaverse. This was good, already. The quote Geoffrey had just read to me had one word, however, that didn't feel right.

'What did he mean by emanated?'

'Spread, diverged. This is only a translation of Maitreya's work, so I would have to see the Tibetan characters to give you an exact meaning.'

'When I move, I don't feel like I'm spreading out through all the other worlds. I can sense them, but I'm definitely in this one.'

'Perhaps that feeling would be different if you had overcome your attachment to particulars. Perhaps, if, like the Buddha, you were as liberated, as unattached, as it was possible for a human being to be, you would simultaneously exist in all universes.'

'Possibly.' I liked this conversation. There was no way I could talk about such things with Zed and Deano. With a quick glance, I gave Tara a smile, to show her my gratitude that she'd brought me here, but she was solemn.

'I don't see how Liam can be like Buddha. He's such a messer and a troublemaker. At school he's ... he's sometimes mean and a bully.'

I must have looked surprised.

'Well, sorry Liam, but it's true and this is important. Anyway,' she turned back to Geoffrey, 'how can he be enlightened? He's never even looked at a Buddhist book before.'

It was slightly hurtful that she still had such a low opinion of me, especially now, when I was trying to see myself in a new light, as a super being. It was pretty cool. Maybe this was how you got to be Jesus or Mohammed or someone that everyone else thought a god. Munching happily on a biscuit, I contemplated my potential divinity.

'Tell me, were you born with this condition?'

Since my mouth was full of chocolate and crumbs, I just shook my head. He waited for me.

'I don't think so. It actually first happened when ... when Tara lost her foot. Originally I was there.' I couldn't look at her now. 'Her scream. I just fled, into a universe where I'd stayed at home that day.'

'A scream?' Geoffrey nodded. 'The Zen Buddhists will like this. They go in for sudden enlightenment, often in the most dramatic of circumstances. What was it you were thinking about at the time?'

'Do you mind?' I lifted my eyes to meet Tara's. She shrugged as if she didn't care. 'It was terrible. Even looking at her foot, well that had made me sick. But the sound of her distress, it's like nothing I've heard since. I had to get out of there. I was desperate and that's when it happened. I opened my eyes and I was at home.'

He frowned. 'Ahh, that's a little disappointing, since it means you are not, after all, an enlightened being.'

'What do you mean?' I glanced again at Tara, who was following our conversation with an intense expression of concentration. What I wanted, apart from to understand my powers, was for her to see that I really was trying; I was going to change, use my ability for the best.

'With all due respect to your suffering, your concern over your own experiences shows great signs of attachment to the world. Let us be generous about your motives and say that it was out of empathy for the pain of Tara that you also were suffering. Even so, all life is suffering. Enlightenment, as I understand it, is not fleeing from pain but reaching a state of existence where you no long exist as a person. You escape the wheel of life, not the sound of a distressed person.'

'Look, I know it sounds a bit feeble, but, really, that was a terrible moment. I honestly don't know how Tara didn't faint. Anyway, that was, like, an unconscious move. It just happened. The next time, I had more choice in the matter.'

'Yes?'

'It happened during a game of football.'

'Football?' Geoffrey chuckled, a friendly sound.

'It was terrible. I'd just missed a sitter – totally embarrassing. I had to get out of there, I was desperate and that's when I saw there were other universes I could go to, places where I had scored and everything was all right.'

Geoffrey, still with a slight smile, shook his head before spreading his fingers over the plastic tablecloth, unconsciously fitting them to the pattern as he spoke. I found myself anxiously awaiting his response.

'Human beings are extraordinary creatures. We have many abilities, not least that we can use our minds to understand the cosmos and ourselves. But we are also extraordinarily good at binding ourselves to illusions through attachments, attachments to things: a house, a car, money.' He waved his hand dismissively and continued, 'or to less material goals, such as nations, or ideas about ourselves, our egos.' Geoffrey paused to take a drink of tea. 'The desire to be admired is a particularly strong illusion.

'Buddha became enlightened through contemplation. Liam learned to see other universes, because his attachments were driving him onwards. These cannot be the same experiences. With all due respect to the feelings of that little boy, being attached to the results of a sporting event, or even to the result of something that seems much more important, such as a war, can never be liberating.'

'I'm not concerned about the football match now. I'm just explaining how it got started.'

'Yes. And I am explaining to Tara here as much as to you why

I don't think your abilities are those of a god.' Tara smiled at the thought of me as a god, but Geoffrey continued in a serious vein. 'Gods would not display such an attachment to earthly considerations. You are a human, albeit a very fortunate one who can see into some of the other worlds. That is a great gift and it should help you achieve an understanding of the cosmos in a way that is much deeper than for most.'

Not a god? Well, that was a very short-lived contemplation on being divine. It had lasted about as long as it took me to eat a biscuit. It was true, though. I knew I was no god. I couldn't imagine Jesus or the disciples loving football as much as I did, or enjoying lying on the sofa on Sundays, watching Formula 1 with my dad. They'd be out and about doing something much more worthwhile, especially on Sundays.

'Tara tells me that you have recently had a very painful experience.'

'Yeah, it's been hell in school this week. No one is speaking to me. They think I sent her this.'

When Geoffrey read the card, he flinched. A moment later, he lifted his deep brown eyes and looked across at Tara with an expression of concern.

'Are you alright?'

'Fine, really. Everyone in class is being so kind to me. It's more than made up for Valentine's Day.'

'Good.' He looked carefully at the card, and then set it down flat on the table.

'There was a card that I'd made for Tara. It was a really cool one, very romantic, even if I do say so myself. I'd put a Persian prince on the front, which I'd cut out from a picture I'd bought in the Chester Beatty Museum. But when I opened my bag to show it to my friend Zed, it had gone.'

Once I had finished explaining myself, there was silence while Geoffrey studied the card again, without picking it up. Up until now I had been feeling quite cheerful. After all, I was with Tara. It was nearly a date, sort of. Then meeting this man had made me think about my ability to move in an interesting way. But there was something about the intense scrutiny that Geoffrey was giving to the card that made me feel cold.

'Do you sense something wrong about it?' I asked him.

He nodded. 'I do.'

'You believe me when I say I can see into nearby universes?'

'Yes.'

'Well, normally every object around me is flowing away from this moment. There are millions of alternatives, even some pretty remote ones where this table itself collapses. Everything is fluid until I fasten on one particular universe – everything, that is, except for that card. It is solid. It has been fixed in some way. It's creepy. It is in all the possible universes I can see. I can't get away from it. There is some kind of intelligence at work here. What happened on Valentine's Day must have been deliberate.'

'Yes,' he murmured solemnly. 'Did you ever meet anyone else like you?'

'Not that I know of.'

'Ever feel yourself exchange universes involuntarily?'

'I don't think so. When I move, I feel dizzy for a moment. It takes a few seconds for my memories to settle down. The only time I've had that feeling is after I've moved from my own choice. I think that if I was somehow made to move, I'd still get the disorientation and the extra memories.'

Neither Tara nor I spoke, but Geoffrey's face became more sombre still.

'Do you have any more examples, like this card, or anything unusual recently?'

'Well, I had a dream like I've never had before. It was really intense. I was starving, forever and ever. But it wasn't food I wanted, it was dark powerful emotions. And I got them. I plunged in, right among them. If I hadn't woken up, I'd still be filling myself with them and the more I felt angry or jealous or guilty, the more I felt I had to keep going, to taste something stronger.'

Speaking like this frightened me and I got no reassurance from the other two. Tara was looking worriedly at Geoffrey, who was pale, his elbows on the table, hands clasped together, pressing on his lips.

'What's the matter?' asked Tara.

'Did you ever read about "hungry ghosts"?'

Tara nodded. 'I did. You don't think a hungry ghost is to blame?'

'Perhaps.'

'But I thought they were just metaphorical.'

'No. They are real.'

As soon as I had heard the words 'hungry ghost', a shiver had run through me. The hairs on my arms had risen and my eyes moistened.

'It seems to me possible that a hungry ghost is among us. In which case this,' he touched the card, 'is just the start.'

'What's a hungry ghost?' Even saying the words was chilling.

'If a being lived a particularly unwholesome life, like a human who habitually tortured and murdered others, they might be re-born as a demon. There are many kinds of demon; the hungry ghosts are the kind which are almost pure destructive appetite. They are depicted in the early texts as having small mouths with giant distended stomachs. Here ...' He got up from the table and picked out a book from his shelves, it was bound in leather and the pages were yellowing. Finding the page he wanted, he put it on the table and my heart stopped.

The sketch was of a demon, teeth razor-sharp, eyes as cold and greedy as those of a shark. The expression on its face was of intense desire and I recognised it at once. Far away a man on a gallows was jerking his body, trying to force the passage of air through the unyielding grip of the rope pulled tight around his throat. That was me. That was how I felt, utterly winded by shock and fear. Echoes of suppressed nightmares surged out of the dark spaces from between the universes and I was drowning in them while the other two simply carried on talking. Did they not see that just looking at the picture had stricken me, bringing tears to my eyes and a raggedness to my breath?

'What does it want?' asked Tara, looking across to Geoffrey, oblivious to my reaction.

'Some, who perhaps were avaricious as humans, want wealth. Others, the gluttons, want food. There are hungry ghosts for every kind of untrammelled desire.'

'And one of them is here among us, seeking negative emotions?'

'So it seems, from Liam's dream and this malicious card.'

'The hungry ghost gave me the card? Why?' Tara was trying to make sense of it all.

'To feed upon the harm it caused to you and Liam.'

'But why me? Why Liam?' She looked at me, her expression turning to surprise, probably at the fact there were the tears in my eyes.

'I don't know.' Geoffrey's voice was soft, concerned.

If Zed or someone else from the class heard us talking like this, they would have thought us crazy. But they hadn't felt the strangeness of the universes that would not let me move away from the card, nor had they experienced my terrible dreams.

Both Geoffrey and Tara were looking at me now and, in the silence, the shock that had overtaken me when I was shown the picture of the hungry ghost was fading.

'Fine.' I suddenly had strength to reach across and close the book, hiding the picture. 'How do we destroy it?'

'Ha!' Geoffrey surprised me by slapping his hand on the table, causing the card to bounce. 'That's the spirit. I admire the bravery of your response. Destroy it. Yes, that's what we will have to find out. In the meantime, I think that we should teach you how to meditate. It can't do you any harm and it might do a lot of good.'

7
Easy Come ...

Uncountable new estates have come into being around Dublin, supplanting the fields and surrounding the city with a ring of pristine toy dwellings. Tara and her family lived in one of these. Rowanstown was about thirty minutes walk from our street, which was way cooler, being in old Cabra and all.

Each time I rang her doorbell, I really hoped that it would not be her parents who answered it. Even with Tara telling them that it wasn't me who sent the card their faces expressed clear disapproval of me.

This time the blurred figure that loomed up through the rippled glass was Tara. Good, although there was still her dog to deal with. Rascal, a little Jack Russell, was a pain, leaping about, barking with enthusiasm. But I had to smile for her sake and pretend to be charmed.

'Come in.'

The three of us went into the front room. It had a polished wooden floor and Rascal scrabbled for purchase as he lashed around, sniffing at my feet and yapping.

'He's excited to see you.'

'So I see.'

Sitting down could not be avoided and, of course, Rascal immediately tried to climb up my legs, panting eagerly. I pushed him aside, gently. He was straight back at it.

'Down, Rascal, down!'

Tara leaned forward apologetically. Her hair was loose and it gathered at her shoulder before the distinct strands cascaded forward to cover her face. She flicked them back with a jerk of her head and our eyes met.

'I'm sorry, Tara. I'm not going to be able to concentrate with Rascal in the room.'

'I know, but let's just get him used to your being here, or he'll be whining at us all night.'

That made sense, so I held out my hand for him to lick and petted him a little.

'What's the plan?' I asked her.

'Meditation first, then try you at some numbers.'

'Numbers are getting boring. It's hard to motivate myself.'

'I know but here.' She rummaged in her bag and pulled out a pink lotto ticket. 'I was wondering: can you change the numbers on this?'

'How do you mean?'

'Can you change universes to one where the numbers here are different?'

Interesting. I tried and there it was. So I moved.

'It worked,' I said.

'Did it? I don't see any change?'

'No, you wouldn't, because you've always been in this universe. But when we began the conversation, I was in one where there was no number 23 on that ticket.'

'Great. I was thinking it might be more fun for you to see the numbers as they're being drawn at eight and try to match them.'

'That's a really good idea.'

'In the meantime, you should do some more meditation.'

'Go on, then.'

It took Tara a few minutes to persuade Rascal to leave the room, and to get two mats to throw down on to the floor. While she was busy with her beloved pet, I stretched out on the luxurious and expensive sofa. It was good to be in her house. I'd come a long way from when I first tried to chat to her. Did she like me now? Did she fancy me even?

One advantage of having a missing foot was that Tara could sit comfortably in the lotus position. The fact that she wasn't shy about unstrapping it in my presence I took as a great compliment. The lotus position was too uncomfortable for me, though. I just sat cross-legged on my mat, something I hadn't done with this kind of regularity since first or second class.

'Concentrate on your breathing. Don't try to alter it, just be aware of it.' Tara was much more practised at meditation than I was.

In and out. In, out. Once I began to think about it, my cycle of breathing became slower, more relaxed.

'Let your thoughts fall away.'

This was the tricky part. Either I felt sleepy, which wasn't the point, or I couldn't control the way that thoughts just popped up. Sometimes fragments of music came to mind, which was deadly, in the bad sense of the word. But more often it was just clutter. Like, I meant to get some new batteries for our TV's remote control, but I'd forgotten on the way over. There was O'Grady's newsagents. I could call into it on the way back; it stayed open late. See? To get away from the junk in my head, I went back to my breathing. In and out. In, out.

This time I became very conscious of the fact that Tara was sitting on her mat, right beside me. Her inhalations were just loud enough to hear and I found that my own breathing slowed, matching hers. Out of the corner of my eye I could see her body and I became aware of her slight motion, a gentle rhythm of life under her cotton T-shirt. The images in my mind were far from empty, tranquil and calm. Instead I was thinking how easy it would be right now to turn to her and kiss her. Then what would happen? Would she freak? Or would she welcome it? Our bodies pressed together, lying together on the floor. Kissing her soft lips. It was a vivid, ecstatic thought. And I could test it. All I had to do was look in to adjacent universes, see what the possibilities were, even move to the one where my imaginings came true. But something held me back. In some way, it felt disloyal to Tara to look at the alternatives. These last few weeks she had been brilliant. If it hadn't have been for her, the class might have kept up their boycott of me for a long time, but she adamantly insisted to anyone who would listen that I hadn't sent her the card. The fact that we hung out a lot was evident to all, and if the main victim of the offence didn't hold a grudge, it was hard for everyone else to.

So, virtuously, I went back to my breathing. This time I focused on the tip of my nose and the feel of the air as I exhaled and inhaled. The sensation of each was very different. A great relaxation sank through me, from my head down to my feet. The presence of Tara beside me was still a strong one, but now it was that of a companion, supportive and calming. For a moment, I had the kind of balance that Geoffrey had talked about when he had explained meditation to me. My sense of time itself was gone. I just existed in a tranquil effortless state, not really thinking at all.

Eventually, thoughts began to return and foremost among them was the lotto idea. Supposing we won it, we would be millionaires, at least in the universe to which I'd moved in order to have the right ticket.

Checking across at Tara, I could see that she was still in a fairly deep meditative state, her eyes were closed, her hands resting, upturned, on her knees, her breathing deep and slow. The pale skin of her cheek looked soft and cool. I could imagine how it would feel if I ran the back of my hand over it. If I were to have a portrait of Tara, it would be with her sitting like this, totally relaxed, except that her grey eyes would be open, looking back at me.

While waiting for her as patiently and as quietly as I could, I listened to the sounds of her house. Somewhere above us, there was classical music being played. Nearby, Rascal was restless, often trotting past the door, sometimes pausing for a sniff. At last Tara's breathing changed and she opened her eyes.

'What time is it?'

I checked my watch. 'Seven fifteen.'

'How did that go, any progress?'

'Yeah, I think so. But maybe I need to do it more on my own.' Her face fell slightly.

'Don't get me wrong. I like being here, meditating beside you, but I'm too aware of you – in a good way.' This was becoming a bit revealing, so I shut up.

'I know what you mean. Being alone is probably best.'

The TV flared up, accompanied by a rush of sound. Tara had pressed the remote control. She flicked around the channels. It was really strange to contrast the blare and restless colour of the images with the recent state of calm and peace we had been in. She settled for 'The Simpsons'.

'Did you ever see the one where Bart solved a great mystery of Zen Buddhism?' I asked her.

'No?' She smiled back, curious.

'You know how the Zen Buddhists like paradoxes?'

'I do.'

'Well, one of theirs is: what is the sound of one hand clapping? One episode, someone asked Bart the question and he said, "That's easy", and he did this.' I flicked the fingers of my right hand against its palm, like I was making a fist, but really fast. It made a definite clapping sound.

'Ha!' Tara laughed gleefully. 'That's brilliant.'

We spent the next while fooling around in this way and, before long, we were pretty good at it. This kept us busy until it was time for the lotto draw.

'Are you ready?' Tara had the ticket. I nodded. 'Here, you hold it.' She passed it over to me.

While I sat in my meditation position, facing the screen, Tara changed channel to where the presenter, Ronan Collins, was briskly explaining the game, his bright teeth gleaming out of a constant smile. As I began to explore the universes in my vicinity, I felt them all, clearer than ever, seething and writhing away from this moment. The colourful balls were released, bouncing around in the transparent box. One came out, 41. It was hard to grasp at alternative universes simply by looking for tiny changes to the markings on the pink paper in my hand. It was easier to find those where my own reactions showed the number was correct.

'That's one,' I announced, having moved to the universe in which I gave the confirmation.

Already the second number was rolling into place, 13.

'That's two.' It was easier this time, knowing I could look for my own voice. Before the next ball came down I was ready. 21.

'Twenty-one,' repeated Ronan Collins from the TV.

'Three,' I added.

12.

'Four.'

37.

'Five.'

4.

'Six.'

This was easiest of all. There were very marked differences between the nearby universes, revealing as if in a bright beam those in which we had got all six numbers, including ones where Tara and I were leaping about hugging each other. Naturally that's the one I moved to.

'Amazing, it's just incredible.' Tara held me tight, for a few glorious seconds, dependent upon me to keep her balance. Then she broke away to look at me, her eyes sparkling. Basking in her admiration, I was taken completely by surprise when her expression became impish and she snatched the ticket from me.

'Just think, this bit of paper is worth two million euro.' She waved it before my face.

'Yeah, cool huh?'

She tore it in half.

'What the ...! I swear to God ... Tara!'

Putting the two pieces of the ticket together, she tore them again, and again. I shut my open mouth, shocked. The winning ticket was a pile of pink fragments in the palm of her hand. She brushed them into a wastepaper basket.

'I don't get it.'

Tara sighed. 'True. You really don't. Can't you see that money is irrelevant? This was a training exercise.'

'So it was. But, like, that's a million each.'

'If you really need money, although I don't see why you should with your ability, you could just do it again, win it for yourself.'

'What about you, though? Don't you want money?'

'It's useful. But if I understand what's happening, you have picked the universe where you won. But in millions of universes, we didn't win, right?'

'True enough.' I could vaguely feel them, fading away from me.

'Well, in some universes we won; in most we lost. Are there any universes where I attack you with a kitchen knife?'

'There are not. Well, I can't check them all, but I doubt it.'

'Same here. And think about Geoffrey, can you see him being cruel? Or violent?'

I didn't know Geoffrey as well as Tara did, but I did know her, so I shook my head.

'See, in some universes you are rich, in others poor, and you can probably swap between them very easily. But what you can't swap, what you, all of us, have to work on, is who we are. And I don't think you would be a better person with a million euro in the bank, do you?'

'I'd be just the same,' I replied resentfully, 'only I could buy a cool place to live, move out from my parents. Also get some decent gear for my band.'

'I'm telling you, Liam. You give yourself things like that for free and you pay a price in terms of your own development. When you are old, and you've had everything you wanted all your life, always side-stepped the problems and difficulties, what kind of person do you think you'll be? You'll be nothing. No one will respect you and you won't respect anyone else. You know what will happen after you die? You'll be a hungry ghost, seeking all the emotions that you never had while you lived.'

Nobody likes being lectured to in this way and I was angry that she thought me so shallow. It wasn't like a load of money would make me a bad person. Winning the lotto had taken a lot of effort, and I was almost annoyed enough to seek out a universe where I hadn't let her grab the ticket. But I let the feeling pass with a shrug.

'Maybe you're right.'

'Don't you think that this is important? That somehow your choices matter?'

'Not really. Lighten up a bit Tara. Moving is a lot of fun.'

She looked worried at this. 'Have you forgotten that card already? Because I haven't.'

8
Mutiny

Not long before our fifth-year exams we were in our English class, with Mr Kenny up the front, sighing over some Gerard Manley Hopkins. It was a very warm day and I was completely tuned out, watching small white clouds drifting across a blue sky. During the lunch break, I'd been playing football, the sun and the game had reminded me of the freedom of the summer holidays. As a result, I was resentful at having to go back in at the bell, and not in the least bit inclined to pay attention to the giant droopy dog up the front. An instant later, though, and my detachment had gone.

'Oww! Christ!' That was me, in immense pain. It was hard to keep my voice down and sit still because of it. Deano and I had this crazy, stupid competition where if we could catch the other person off guard, we gave them a dig with our heels into their shins. His was the desk on my left and seeing as I am left-footed and he was right-footed, it was a fair game. If the other person was daydreaming, as I had been, you could reach out your leg, line it up on their shin and give them a sharp backheel. Usually the distance and the angle meant that it was not easy to get a really hard blow in, but I'd been distracted enough to let Deano come half out of his desk and deliver a vicious one. I'd have a massive bruise there, right on the bone, no question. His grin was slightly nervous; he knew how bad it had been.

'Mr O'Dywer, have you something to share with the class?'

'No, sir.'

'And yet I am convinced that I heard an exclamation from your direction. Can you explain that?'

'No, sir.'

'Curious. We shall continue in the hope that you can subdue your passion for poetry.'

For the next ten minutes we had to act as model students, all diligence and alertness. In any case, there was no point trying to get Deano back straight away; he'd be on guard. But when Dog Face was asking Debbie Healy about the significance of the alliteration of 'barrowy brawn', I felt my chance had come. It was a good old kick, but something was wrong, I didn't feel shinbone against my heel and there was no suppressed yelp from Deano. In fact, he was grinning a big wide toothy smile. As I looked at him, half intrigued, but half angry with thwarted vengeance, Deano raised his trouser leg. Tucked into his sock was a shin pad.

'Cheatin' rat,' I whispered. He put his head down and pretended to be reading his book. The longer I glared at him, the more his shoulders began to shake. Soon he was wracked with chuckles, unable to meet my eyes, delighted at being one up on me. His mirth overcame my righteous indignation at his cheating, and it set me off too, anger giving way to laughter. Our giggles were irresistible, especially given that we had to keep an eye on Mr Kenny, who was extolling in passionate phrases the sonnet we were studying. Each time I felt the laughter had passed and my lungs were able to take in a deep draught of air, I would look over at Deano, whose moist eyes were sparkling with the effort of containing himself. He would look at me and we would start chuntering again. It was a dangerous game and that, precisely, was why it was so funny.

'Mr Dywer, you are amused by this sonnet? You find Hopkins displaying humour in it? Would you care to elucidate your insight for the benefit of us all?'

'No, sir.'

'I rather thought not.' Mr Kenny walked down the aisle of the desks to stand between Deano and me. Never did he look more canine than when he sank his jaw deep in the jowls of his chin in order to look down at us.

'What's this?' He pointed to a picture of a ploughman that accompanied the poem in my book. Some previous owner had drawn all over the ploughman's face, adding huge ears, glasses, a moustache and a beard. I didn't reply. I just kept my head down. After a short pause in which we held our positions, Mr Kenny turned on his heel, to walk slowly back up to the front of the room. This was slightly worrying. An outburst would have meant that the issue was over.

'Class Five A2. Books are a valuable human inheritance. A book is like a chalice that contains the most precious substance of all, knowledge. Properly treated, books will last centuries, passing on the thoughts and emotions of our forebears. To treat your books disrespectfully is to belittle the efforts and achievements of some of the greatest literary minds. Liam O'Dwyer, come up to the front of the classroom please.'

'Sir?'

'You heard me. And bring your book.'

This was bad, as Zed made clear from the wide-eyed expression he gave me during my long walk up through the desks. Right from the start of the year we'd been kept apart, Zed put up the front, me at the back.

'Show the class what you did.'

'What, sir?'

'Show the class what you did to your book!' His voice became angrier, a flush crossed his cheek.

'The drawing, sir? That was in the book when I got it.'

'You, O'Dwyer, are a philistine and a liar. I saw you and Kirwan laughing at your picture. Five A2, you have among you someone who would spit on one of English literature's most sensitive souls, spit, I say, on a man who poured his life into his writing, only to have uncouth louts like O'Dwyer draw filthy pictures all over his poems. How would you feel if your book was scribbled on with such disrespect?'

This was getting to the point where I was fed up. Not only

was I innocent but Mr Kenny's hatred of me had led him into making a very pompous rant. I began to search around for a universe to move into, just a plain, simple, boring literature class with no fuss, when I suddenly felt dizzy with an involuntary move. The feeling was as nauseating as Mr Kenny's self-righteous lecture.

'O'Dwyer.' Mr Kenny stood up and leant right over me, face ferocious. 'Give me your pen.'

'What, sir?' All the time I was scrambling around to find a universe that would allow me to duck out of this scene. Horribly, they were all closed off to me, shrouded in darkness; only those with the frothy-mouthed teacher could be seen. Thrashing around in them was like drowning.

'Your pen.'

There was no escape, which was something even more frightening than the fact that Mr Kenny had lost the run of himself. I handed him my biro.

'Here's a lesson for you, O'Dwyer. How would you like to be written upon, to be mocked?'

The pen shot out at me and drew a mark above my lip. The class went totally silent, horrified.

'Stand still boy!' Mr Kenny's shout was ferocious and his hand grabbed the hair at the back of my head, holding me in place. The pen hurt as it covered my chin, my cheeks. Around my eyes he drew circles for glasses. At last, he released me, stepping back to admire his handiwork. My face burned, not with pain but humiliation. Never had I been so ashamed. Tears came to my eyes and it was even harder to check them when I saw intense satisfaction in Mr Kenny's expression. Frustration and anger welled up inside me. If I could have found a universe where the roof fell on his head and killed him, I would have moved to it. But everything was closed to me, everything except this moment, this suffering.

The bell rang and Mr Kenny promptly swept out of the room, leaving a totally stunned class behind him. No one even coughed.

At last I felt an arm on my shoulder. It was Zed.

'Come on, mate. Let's try to get that off.'

He steered me out and down to the toilets.

'What a lunatic. That's gotta be illegal. What a complete gobshite.' Zed was trying to console me, but I was so shocked and outraged I couldn't speak.

It took a while for the shame and anger to subside. When it did, I found a very different emotion creeping up on me: fear. Someone had trapped me in that moment, bound me even more tightly than the day of the Valentine's card, and if they could do that, what else could they do?

***

The way Mr Kenny had gone to town on me probably fuelled what happened two days later. Our form teacher was Mr Brown, the French teacher. He was strict, but pretty fair, so we had a certain amount of respect for him. One morning, as he took the register, Hazel Cartwright put her hand up.

'Hazel?'

'Sir, when are we getting information about our class trip?'

'Ahh.' Mr Brown closed the register and stood up. 'I'm sorry to say that since there were no volunteers to take you, there will be no class trip.'

This news was a shock and an audible murmur spread around the class. All fifth-year classes got a trip away, usually to Paris or some European city. Of course we had to pay, but it was supposed to be great craic, at least that's what all the sixth years told us. Some of our class had been saving already, even though we didn't know where we were off to.

'Sir?' Hazel called out to him just as he was reaching for the door.

'Hazel?'

'Why don't you take us?'

'I dislike class trips. But as it happens I felt sorry for you all and did offer that if another member of staff would accompany us, I would be willing to take you, providing our destination was in France.' He looked at us over his glasses. 'Unfortunately your reputation is such that my offer was declined.'

With that, Mr Brown hurriedly left the room, perhaps a little ashamed about the betrayal of our class by the other teachers, or perhaps he felt he had been indiscreet in telling us about the attitude of his colleagues. It was understandable of course, and I was as much to blame as anyone. Actually, I was more to blame than the others. I've told you how being able to move allowed me to terrorise Mr Kenny. Well, there was other stuff too.

We used to have 'morning prayer' at our school. One of the nuns, usually Sister Rita, would speak through the tannoy system before registration, offering us a few thoughts every day, about who should be in our prayers. She was good on the stories of saints and also on reminding us about those worse off than ourselves. Soon after the start of fifth year, Zed and I had gone to her and explained that we wished to do the 'morning prayer'. It wasn't easy, but I had moved us to a universe in which she had agreed. For two weeks we played it dead straight, even looking up information in the saints' calendar, but then we started to push it a bit.

'Friends, today we would like you to remember in your prayers the people who make the little bolts that attach the school radiators to the walls. It is easy to overlook such small devices, but they are indispensable to the whole system. Without them, we would not be warm in winter. So when you say your prayers this morning, please give a thought to those who work day after day in their factories around the world, making small screws and bolts. They too deserve our thanks.'

That kind of invitation to prayer can go on for a long time if you say it right, with proper sincerity. While I was fairly good at it, Zed was pure genius. His speciality was in making up new responsibilities for the saints, like Saint Cuthbert, the patron saint of dinner ladies. In some ways it was amazing that we lasted nearly a month before we were brought before the head-master and slaughtered. Although we never really said anything too bad, the whole school had caught on to us and were laughing throughout prayer; our mates were dying to see what we would say next. By the end of the month, even the dimmest of the teachers had figured it out and we were busted.

It was that kind of activity which was rebounding against us. I could go on, but the point was that our class now felt a huge sense of injustice. Even though I had lost a lot of ground over the Valentine's card, everyone was sickened by what Mr Kenny had done to me. On top of that came the shocking news that we weren't getting a trip away. Funnily enough, it was those in the class who were usually the quietest who got the most worked up. After registration we had double history with Miss McClernnas, who was decent enough, but we couldn't concentrate.

'Five A2, will you settle down?' She kept stopping the lesson to call out to us in her northern accent. 'What's got into you all?'

Hazel put her hand up. 'Miss, why won't you take us on our trip?'

'Take you lot? Why I wouldn't take you down the park, let alone out of the country. God knows what you'd be up to.' She laughed, but we didn't.

Miss McClernnas was very sober by the time she left us, closing the door behind her with a shake of her head. No sooner had she gone than Hazel Cartwright picked up her desk and carried it over to the door. The three fifth-year classes are in a wing together. There is one corridor that connects the rooms to the main body of the school. Usually we barrelled out at morning break, because it only lasted fifteen minutes, but today Hazel stopped us.

'Bring your desks.'

She made us take them out into the corridor and pile them up against the one door that led to the rest of the school. Once we got into the idea, we did a pretty good job.

'The side door.' Jocelyn led the way to where a door led out to the back field.

'Wait.' Debbie Healy and two of her friends went into Five B and we could just about hear them. 'All of you had better get out. We're blocking the doors.'

'Yeah, good idea.' Zed went to Five C. Deano and I came along. 'Hey, you lot. Grab everything you want and get out, because we're taking over.'

By this time, the corridor was full of curious fifth years.

'Hurry, hurry!' We hustled the other classes along. It was time for our moment of revenge. Once our blood was up, we got into the mutiny properly, finding that the big cupboards were amazingly light when you had lots of people lifting them. There was no question of anyone getting into the building once we'd put those massive obstacles up against the doors. Personally, what surprised me the most was seeing Hazel leading it all. It was like watching Barbie rioting.

'This is deadly,' Zed muttered as we tested the barricade, and I had to agree. We'd never done anything like it before; no class I knew had done anything like this.

Up until the end of break, we had all been loud and excited, stopping to ask each other: 'how long are we doing this for? What are we going to demand?' As soon as the bell rang, though, we fell silent. Most of us returned to our own class-room. It felt wide and empty with nothing but our chairs and bags in it.

Thump! Thump! The teachers had realised they were blocked

out and were trying to budge the doors. No chance. All the same, we rushed back out to the barricades to check.

The other fifth classes were milling around the windows, jumping up to see what was going on. They were making a lot of noise, as if break time were still going on. It was when they suddenly went quiet that we knew the teachers were outside.

The Monk, the headmaster himself, was visible through a window in Five C. We had inherited the nickname from those years which had gone before us and had called him it, probably on account of his ragged beard. Although, there was a criminal too, in Dublin, a gang leader, and maybe he'd got the title that way.

'Liam O'Dwyer, I see you. Come and open this door right now!'

I nipped out of sight.

'Cover up the windows!' ordered Hazel, and soon the ledges were filled with our bags, preventing the teachers from seeing inside.

The rest of the day flew by. Each time we checked our watches, we'd say, 'That's geography gone', or 'that's chemistry over'. The teachers were pleading with us through the doors and windows, saying we were only hurting ourselves, reminding us of the coming exams. Michael Clarke and a few others were going around saying we should end it. They were afraid of being expelled. But we pointed out to them that if we all stuck together, the school just couldn't expel everyone.

For a while the Monk tried reasoning with us, with Hazel shouting back through the door in response to his questions.

She kept demanding that the school promise us a trip away, but all the headmaster would do was point out that our undisciplined behaviour was exactly why no one would take us. He did promise to look into the issue, providing we took down the blockade, but only the doubters were willing to settle for that.

The best fun was imagining the reaction of the rest of the school. At break time they all must have come over to our buildings to see it for themselves, because we could hear the excited chatter outside. It was pretty amazing really, for us to be doing this, I could hardly believe it. I hadn't even had to move to get to this universe. Here it was; strange things do happen on their own.

Finally, at quarter to four, we put everything back. The teachers had given up trying to get in, so they didn't even notice. At final bell, we walked out proudly, congratulating each other.

'Good job, Hazel.'

'You too, Zed.'

There was a group of our teachers standing beside the Monk, watching us as we left.

'Liam O'Dywer, in my office, now.' The headmaster's voice was quiet, quiet but full of menace. The rest of the teachers looked pretty grim too, with the possible exception of Mr Brown, whose eyes were twinkling as though he were suppressing a smile. Did he approve of our protest? I hoped so, but I couldn't expect any help from him. I was going to be in big trouble and it was time to search the universes to see if I could find a way out.

'Sir, Liam had nothing to do with it.' Unexpectedly, Hazel

stepped up to my side. A bunch of my classmates had stopped to watch. I have to say, even now, writing about it, I get goose-bumps when I think about the way she spoke out on my behalf. You have to bear in mind that I had nothing to lose really. My parents were used to me being in trouble. But Hazel, she had never been in trouble in her life. If her parents had seen her that day, they would have freaked. Trying to defend me was brave, much braver than anything I had ever done, because of course I could always move out of real hassle. Or at least I could have until recently.

'Hazel Cartwright, go on home.' The Monk glowered at her.

'But, sir, it's not fair to pick on Liam.'

'It's all right, Hazel. You go on, please.' Only for the sincerity of my voice did she back down.

'You too, Dean Kirwan.'

To save anyone else from getting themselves into trouble, I set off for the headmaster's office. He quickly followed and the small group of teachers and my classmates broke up.

Once inside the Monk's office, he had me stand in front of his desk, while he looked over my file, out and ready-to-hand.

'Not long ago, O'Dwyer, you wouldn't have been able to sit for a week after that disgraceful exhibition.' He glared at me as if inviting me to read his thoughts and the violence in them. I looked straight back at him but I said nothing.

'Who else was involved? Zimraan Nouri? Dean Kirwan?'

Of course I didn't reply.

'You are only making things worse for yourself.' He shook his head. 'You know I can expel you for this? Answer me, boy.'

'Yes, sir.' Actually, I thought that he could expel me at any time. Did he need to give a reason? Were there constraints on him?

'Sit down.'

He picked up the phone and tapped out a number. It was my home.

'Mrs O'Dwyer? Mr Hance here. Yes, the headmaster ... It is ... He's in a great deal of trouble and I would appreciate it if you could come here right away. Thank you.'

The Monk then began a long lecture, recalling my troubled record in its entirety. His theme was appreciation versus ingratitude, but I wasn't paying attention. My thoughts were on my mum. She would be worried as she drove over. Almost without thinking, I began to slide into that state from which I could see the nearby universes and move. But I stopped myself. For once, I had done nothing wrong, and, even though I was nervous, I was proud too, in a way, for taking the blame and protecting the others.

What's more, it all worked out all right. The Monk told my mum that he had considered expelling me, but that instead I was on my final warning. I think he expected me to get hell at home. But once Mum and I were alone, I could tell her the God's honest truth: that I hadn't started the blockade or done anything more than the rest of my class. She glanced at me from time to time as we drove home, and she believed me.

Dad was great too. He just laughed when he heard about it.

'Jaysus! I wished we'd have done that when I was in school. Mind you, in our day we'd have been beaten black and blue for pulling a stunt like that.'

Strangely, from that day I was as popular as ever with my class, and I had earned their friendship without having to move. All this time, deep inside, I thought that the reason everyone admired me was because I'd moved to places where I looked impressive. I felt that they didn't really know me and, if they did, they'd find out that, instead of wild devil, I was really a shy, indoors, kind of boy. Some part of me was still on that barge, being sick. That day, the famous day of the takeover of the fifth-year block, I won some respect from my class but more importantly, for the first time, I began to get some belief in myself that had nothing to do with being able to move.

9

Hunted or Hunter?

It troubled me that I hadn't really told my best friend anything about my abilities or my fears. The problem with opening my heart to Zed was that it might damage our friendship. As far as he was concerned, Zed was the top dog and I was the sidekick. Zed enjoyed being the one to decide what we would do, who we would see. He liked explaining stuff to me: what music was cool, what clothes to wear, that kind of thing.

One of the reasons I'd hung back from proving that I could move was that it risked changing things between us. Would he admire my ability, or resent it? But I had to tell him. I needed his help.

One day after school, Zed and I were in town to try out the new games in the computer shop. We were walking alongside the walls of Trinity College when it occurred to me that this time was as good as any.

'Hey, Zed, let's go into Trinity.'

'What for?'

'It's quiet there and I need to talk to you about something.'

The college is an oasis of calm at the centre of the busy streets of Dublin. Stepping through the great doors of the entrance is like entering a different world, one of space, light and peace. Stately buildings form the boundaries of great squares of cobblestone or lawn. When you are walking past the libraries, the croquet lawns and the playing fields, it's easy to forget that outside the walls of the college is a restless noisy city.

It was also a really good place to go skateboarding, until about three months earlier that year, when the security got very heavy about it.

We settled on a bench, watching the students and feeling young because of our uniforms. The girls looked good, but way too old for us and instead of being our usual cocky selves, we sheepishly kept our eyes down.

'What's up mate?'

'Something real serious. Really amazing, but also it might be really bad.' And I told him the whole story, from the first time I moved on the barge day, which he remembered as being weird, through to the Valentine's card, the nightmares and then the other day, when I'd been involuntarily moved to the universe where Mr Kenny had drawn on my face and I couldn't get away. After rushing through my story, relieved to be letting it out, I then, of course, had to prove it all with the numbers trick.

It took ages to overcome Zed's scepticism and I was exhausted when I was done. Suppose I was doing this trick with you, guessing numbers, how many times would I have to do it before you'd begin to believe me? Well for Zed it was, like, the best part of an hour and I had to do really difficult things, such as have a piece of paper blow past saying, 'It's all true.' You can appreciate that there are not many universes where this happens right on cue, so I was in bits by the end. All the time I was watching his face and that, at least, was an amusing distraction from my efforts. Zed is very expressive, and I could visibly see disbelief change to amazement and excitement, then back to concern when I told him about the hungry ghost.

'Wow, this is so cool.'

'Yeah, it's pretty cool alright, in general, but I'm worried it is all going pear-shaped.'

'Right.' He rubbed his thumb across his chin, thoughtfully. 'Why not find a universe where you never jumped in the first place? That way no harm has been done.'

'Believe me, I've tried. It's way too far away.'

'What do you mean?'

'Well, every second, there are thousands of new branches, right?'

'Yeah, I got that.'

'Well, suppose you started over there.' I pointed to the other side of the grass square. 'And as you were coming this way, at every inch you had a thousand new branches. How many branches would you have by the time you got over here?'

'Millions, billions.'

'Exactly. And most of them lost in the dark. I can only see the nearest universes and a few minutes' worth of each at most, before they roll on by.'

'That's a bit rubbish then.' Zed smiled.

'Yeah, shame I can't see more, or Ireland would have won the World Cup by now.'

'Hah, that would be awesome.'

'Actually, if I went to the games, I could probably swing it. But it would be hard work.'

'Brilliant! Let's do it! What else can you do? Could you make us rich?'

'Zed, listen to me. I'm getting into deep trouble with this. Something really nasty is on the loose, some real bad demon. And it's after me. The more I mess around, the worse it's getting.'

He pulled a face at this and turned his attention to the girls walking past.

'You know what I'd do. I'd use it to score some hot babes.'

This made me smile and I simply raised an eyebrow.

'You crafty bollix! You didn't!' Zed sprang up. 'With who?'

'Not telling.'

'You didn't! You did! Jaysus, Liam, I wish I could do that.'

Which was all very well, but I wasn't out to impress Zed. I was trying to get him on side.

'Zed, I need your help.'

He could hear the sincerity in my voice and sat down.

'All right, you think this demon sent the Valentine card?'

'Yeah.'

'And you think it trapped you that time Mr Kenny wrote on your face?'

'Right.'

'Is it invisible?'

'I don't know. I don't think so. I think it looks like a monster, with a massive belly and a tiny mouth full of sharp teeth.'

'So where is it now?' Zed looked over his shoulder and I would have laughed, but it was a good question.

'Maybe in hell?'

'Er, mate, hell? Since when do you believe in hell?'

'Since I had a demon stalk me. Anyway, maybe not hell, but not in our universe. It's as though every time I've moved I've torn a little hole here and there. Until now there are enough gaps for the demon to get through, like, from outside the universe or something.'

'Weird, but, going with it for now, any chance of closing the holes?'

'Maybe. Maybe if I leave off moving, maybe they'll heal up of their own accord.'

'Well, try that then.'

'Yeah, I will, but I have this terrible feeling it's too late.'

'Naaa. Don't you worry. We'll beat it.'

Strangely, even though Zed hadn't offered me anything practical to do, his positive attitude made me feel a lot better. That is, until I saw him scrunching up his face into the strangest distorted looks of pain I'd ever seen.

'Zed, what are you doing?'

'I'm trying to jump universes.'

'Well don't. Didn't you hear anything I was saying? It's bad. Something really bad is happening.'

At least he had the decency to look a bit sheepish at my aggrieved tone.

'Well,' he shrugged, 'let's think about it again. You don't actually know very much about this demon, right? Just dreams and the feeling you got when you saw the picture.'

'Yeah.'

'We need more info, mate. How can we fight it unless we know what we are up against?'

'True.'

'Tell you what. Why don't you move universes to one where you find out what it is that's giving you grief?'

I thought about this and looked into the alternatives that were streaming away from us.

'I don't know. I don't think there is one. There is something though …'

'Yeah?'

'I can feel its presence out there. I guess I could move towards it.' I spoke with great reluctance.

'Go for it!'

'To be honest, Zed, I'm scared. Whatever it is, it's very strong and very evil.'

'Don't let it hunt you. Let us become the hunters.'

'Yeah.' Yeah, right. Become the hunters. It sounded good and I wanted to believe that we could. So I did try.

What happened next was a bit like a dream, because a lot of my attention was in the nearby universes. As I moved towards my fears, I felt scared, but also that I was glad to be doing something at last, that I was taking back some control of the situation.

'Follow me.'

Zed didn't ask why; he just got up. All around us the weather was changing dramatically, becoming darker and darker. People flickered in and out of existence like a pop video speeding up hours of film to just a few minutes. But overall their numbers grew less as I pushed my way through the barriers between universes. The further I moved towards the demon, the emptier the world became.

Soon I was in a universe where only Zed was with me. I'd kept track of him and made sure to move to places where I was both nearer the demon and still with my friend. It meant I wasn't moving directly towards my enemy but circling around, spiralling in towards a terrible darkness. If there came a point where I couldn't get any closer and still have Zed with me, I would stop and try to go back to a happier universe. I couldn't do this on my own.

We were inside the library shop now, where there should have been staff and security guards; all was eerily quiet.

'The demon is close. I think this might be a mistake. I should go back.'

'It's pretty creepy alright.' I don't think Zed had thought seriously about what it meant to go searching for a hungry ghost. Now, though, he was as oppressed as I was by the gloom that was gathering around us. Outside, the fiercest purple clouds I'd ever seen filled the sky, turning the day to dusk.

'Here.' Zed took down two ornamental brass swords that were on the wall, for sale to tourists, and gave me one. 'Push on.'

'Up these stairs.'

As soon as we had ascended a short staircase into the Long Room Library, I felt the tangible presence of the hungry ghost and the hairs all over my body rose up. There was no need to move any more. It was in this universe and close, very close.

The library was a huge room, with a tall roof of curved wooden arches. Between each archway was a dark alcove full of ancient books, and either side of us a row of these alcoves stretched into the distance, as if they would eventually meet at a black point, infinitely far away.

'It's here.'

Zed looked around in every direction, his flimsy sword wavering.

'Where?' He was terrified. His eyes were stretched open wide and his face was paler than I'd ever seen it before.

It didn't help us that beside each alcove was an alabaster bust of a famous scholar. These white heads, with their blank eyes, looked like the decapitated victims of a horrible fiend. They had been drained of all colour and life.

We continued on towards the darkness at the far end of the library. I heard two footfalls, as though at the same time as I had taken a step, someone had also taken a step towards me.

'Did you hear that?' I whispered.

'What?' Zed's nervous voice was barely audible, swallowed up in the immense silence that filled the musty hall.

'A footstep.'

Again. It happened again. With a backward glance, I sent Zed a look of enquiry, but he just shook his head.

I took another step, then a few more, nearly on tiptoes to keep the noise of my footfall to a minimum. The sounds of the other person were getting closer and louder. But strangely Zed gave no indication of hearing them. He was lagging behind me now, as I stopped just short of the corner of one of the alcoves.

My next step would take me around the bookshelf and into view of the hungry ghost, I was sure of it. My legs were shaking and even if I had wanted to run away, I doubt I could have made them work properly. In any case, there's no way I could have turned my back on the monster.

How long did we stand there, unable to look around the corner but equally unable to flee? Perhaps only five minutes, but it felt like hours. At last, a change came over me and, all at once, I couldn't stand being afraid any more. I'd rather face death than prolong this torture of my fast-beating heart. I stepped forward and looked to my left, into the alcove.

It was empty, just a mirror at the far end with my reflection.

***

My reflection looked up and smiled a very wicked smile, eyes glittering with dark joy.

***

At last, a body, a world. O I shall fill my emptiness with these humans! Show me your shame, your fear, your acts of rage and despair. Let me feast, O let me feast!

***

A moment later, I was looking up at Zed.

'Are you all right, mate? You scared me, but you're just kidding right?'

'I dunno. Did I faint?'

'Yeah.'

'Did you see the demon, in the mirror?'

At this Zed looked up, puzzled.

'What mirror?'

It was true; there was no mirror. As I tried to go back over those last few minutes, my thoughts were a complete jumble. I hadn't exactly fainted. What I had felt was that I was sinking through terribly cold, black waters. Far beneath me were worlds of demons, worlds that I desperately wanted to escape. Thrashing all my limbs as though I was swimming, I'd struggled back up to consciousness and Zed.

There was something else as well: a double memory, like I always got after I moved. While I could remember struggling not to sink towards a dark demon realm, I was also aware of rushing up giddily towards a world rich with the scents of food. Back then, when I came around, I couldn't explain what this was, this feeling of being in two places at the same time, but later I would understand exactly what had happened to me that day.

'So, is it still close?' Zed was keeping watch.

'No. It's gone.'

'Really?'

'Really.' But where had it gone? Something inexplicable had just happened to me and, whatever it was, I felt my battles with the hungry ghost were only going to get worse.

10

At Swim, One Boy

Every year our school has a show. The big hall is filled with the entire student body, sitting in rows that seem unusually neat and respectful for a concert audience due to the fact that we are all in uniform. Standing by the walls of the room, teachers slowly track us with watchful attention, like security cameras, knowing that if we get bored we will get restless. Then, it's up to the older classes to entertain the highly sceptical audience.

Sometimes the show is pretty good, like when there are bands on. Often, though, it is awful: Miss Day's recorder class springs to mind. This year Five A2 had a couple of acts. Some of the class, including Tara, were doing a spoof news programme. After them on the program was 'Inextreme'. That was our band, Zed, Deano and me. We were going to do a version of

'Gangsta's Paradise', a really good kick-ass punk version.

All day, we had worn woolly hats, which people had assumed was part of our act, but really it was because we had been at Zed's house the previous night and had used his older brother's electric razor to shave our heads close, with the remaining fuzz forming neat designs. The school was in for a shock when we hit the stage.

Standing in the wings, the three of us were impatient to get on, with Zed and Deano acting like stars and making dismissive comments about what was currently happening in front of us. The girls had a mock news studio set up and actually I thought they were pretty funny. The audience liked them too and were laughing at an interview between the reporter, Tara, and Michael Clarke, who was pretending to be the Monk. Michael was stuttering in horror as he responded to the news that the government had abolished homework. When they finished there was generous applause. The stagehands ran on to clear away their props while Mr Kenny went up to the microphone.

'Next we have another performance from Five A2. Brace yourself for something extreme from our latest pop group: 'Inextreme!'

'Hats off, here we go.' Zed led the way on to the stage and set up behind the drums. I plugged in my guitar and faced out towards the upturned and expectant faces. There were whistles and laughs as people saw our near-bald heads.

'1, 2, 3, 4.' Zed clicked his drumsticks together and he and Deano set up the backline.

At first it was a total blast; we were having exactly the desired effect. The kids were rocking, the teachers looked concerned, especially the headmaster, and Mr Kenny was scowling. We ruled. I looked over to where Tara had left the stage, in the hope that she had stayed to watch. Just as the thought occurred to me that the lyrics of the song were curiously appropriate to my situation, I felt the odd wrench that comes with a move.

My guitar was hopelessly out of tune and I was hitting all the wrong notes. In fact, I had forgotten what the right chords were. This was awful. I had to stop. Deano and Zed were keeping up their parts, but I was stuck.

'Dude, what's going on?' Zed hissed at me. Deano just looked down at his feet and shook his head. Eventually they had to halt too.

'Boo! You suck!'

'Extreme garbage!'

From glory we faced humiliation. Our whole bald-headed thing just called attention to us and, worse, it was going to continue to do so for weeks, until our hair grew out again. The entire school was watching as we made a complete hash of our show. Now their entertainment was in trying to drive us off stage by jeering and shouts. This was rapidly becoming the most embarrassing moment of my life. The look of satisfaction on Mr Kenny's face made me furious. He saw me glaring at him and raised his eyebrows, as if to say: well, what next?

What next was that I was not going to accept this without a fight. Unlike with the Valentine card, and the shock when Mr Kenny drew on my face, I was ready to strike back. Weeks of practice at meditation meant I didn't panic. I could calm myself and see my way out of this universe.

The hungry ghost was close. I could feel its implacable enmity and its rejoicing in my humiliation. It was hard to concentrate, with that evil presence in my mind and the growing sounds of mass derision from in front of me. It didn't help that Zed was shouting at me too, so I closed my eyes. All the alternate universes that I could see were equally bad; this is what I'd expected, but it was still disheartening that the ghost was powerful enough to block me in completely. Still, I was much better at moving than on Valentine's Day, and much more prepared to respond to the crisis.

Out there in the darkness was a universe in which Inextreme had continued with a great performance. We were still playing, less than a minute had passed. It took more effort than I'd ever before put into moving, but eventually I found a cluster of universes where all seemed well. Trying to focus on them was like trying to read a small sign on a train that was rapidly moving away, having to run at a sprint, ignoring everything around me, looking at the sign, bringing it into focus, making sense of it. It was nearly there. I could almost touch it. I could make out some words. Then, with a sickening jerk, I was taken hold of and flung through millions of universes. It was as though all the time I had been striving for the ones I wanted, I had been running in a harness attached to a long thick elastic band. That elastic had violently pulled me away from my desired goal and I had rolled out of control through millions of possibilities.

My head was whirling. Where was I? Not in the large hall at all, but in our classroom along with everyone else. When I put a hand to my head I felt hair. Everyone was crowded around the windows, crying out with amazement.

'They've got it this time.'

'No way, look at it go.'

An extraordinary roar shook the whole school. It was the deep reverberating call of an angry elephant. By standing on a desk like Deano was doing, I could look over my classmates to get a view of the events outside. In the courtyard that was formed on three sides by our school buildings was an elephant. A tattered streamer lay on the ground: 'Fossett's Circus'. Men, presumably from the circus, were trying to appease the elephant, which swayed its head ominously.

'Mad stuff,' observed Deano.

'Hey, Deano. Isn't the school show today?' I asked, still bewildered by the way I had been thrown here.

My question made him take his eyes off the spectacle outside and he turned to me with amazement.

'Man, that's next week. Remember, the Monk postponed it. Good job it wasn't today, hey? We'd have been upstaged by this guy.'

'Deano, you know about our plan to shave our heads?'

'Yeah?' His attention was back on the courtyard, where one of the handlers had the elephant by its ear and seemed to be able to exert some control over it.

'I don't think it's such a good idea. If something goes wrong, it'll make us look pretty daft for weeks.'

'What could go wrong?'

'Well, my amp could go, or yours. Or anything.'

'Could do, I suppose. I don't really mind either way.' There was nothing more to see from our angle so he got off his desk and ran his hand through his fringe, to spike it up a bit. 'Come on though, Liam; just think how Dog Face will freak. It's gotta be worth it for that.'

'True mate, but let's just weigh it up before we make fools out of ourselves.'

Deano just shrugged.

***

That afternoon I was exhausted and panicking. The hungry ghost had tried to pin me to a horrible, embarrassing experience and while I had broken out of that hold, it had been at the cost of being flung around, completely out of control. Was it always going to be like this from now on? It was terrifying to think that the hungry ghost was just going to keep after me, draining me, forcing me to taste shame, pain, fear and who knew what misery? The nature of the hungry ghost meant it wasn't going to let up. I felt that for certain. If only I'd listened to my doubts when I'd first moved, then I wouldn't be in this situation.

My miserable state of mind wasn't improved by the bus journey home, because as soon as I took my seat I began to drowse from mental exhaustion. There, in my dreams, I was subject to another terrible journey through the dark underside of the metaverse. While I was submerged in those frightening oceans, something happened which I'll write about here, although I didn't experience it at the time. It's a reconstruction, but, looking back, there's a part of me knows how to put this down exactly as it happened.

*** *** ***

Ahh, planet Earth, so good to be back, and so much better that I am no longer human. Is there any place like it in the metaverse? I think not. Six billion or so human beings and all mine to feast upon. Especially those gathered here, in this city. Perhaps there are other parts of the planet where there is greater distress and sorrow, stronger emanations that would provide me with greater sustenance. But the people on the streets of this city will serve me well.

Departing the bus, I placed myself at the heart of the throng, by leaning against the wall of a bridge while the humans streamed past in both directions. The experience was immediately rewarding. They did not meet my lustrous hungry eyes, or if they did, they ducked their heads sharply. Too late, though, for I had delved into their emotions and sought out the shame, fear, cowardice, greed and hate that I needed to fill me and to give me the strength to remain on the planet.

So many people, like several herds of cattle travelling in different directions, all trying to pass through the same field. I intended to become powerful enough to carve them apart for the energy I need, to crush them under the weight of their own weaknesses, but as I was newly born and yet to have my full powers, I settled for what came to me freely.

While the planet's yellow star began to descend towards the

head of the river, I inhaled and inhaled, obtaining one particular flavour of replenishing energy that flowed from nearly everybody that passed me: anxiety.

Oh how anxious they were, all these souls. Packed together in their hundreds, almost brushing against one another as they filled the pavements. Yet divided from each other to the point where they felt distaste and even fear from the touch of a stranger. If I were in a harsher environment, where the human beings were struggling against deathly cold or ferocious heat, there would be none of this emptiness and despair. A city is an excellent home for a creature like me.

What did they worry about? Money. Appearance. Status. An elderly man passed and I followed in his wake, for the trail of rage and frustration that poured out of him was strong. The world was leaving him behind and he had done nothing with his life. Inside a dry cleaners he leaned on the counter for support.

'Is it collection?' A young Chinese girl worked behind the till.

'Don't hurry me!' The old man glared at her and she quailed at the unexpected ferocity in his voice. Under his breath he swore at her, just loud enough that she could hear it. They waited then in silence and the longer the moment, the more her confusion grew as to what was expected of her. This was the effect that the old man wished to create and he savoured it as he continued to mutter. Nor did she get any reassurance from the fact that I stared avidly and with evident pleasure at the rheumy eyes of my man.

'Do you have ticket?' Finally, she dared to speak up, encouraged by the fact that another customer had entered the shop.

My man spat out another obscenity, but internally he was intimidated by the newcomer and could no longer outstare the girl behind the counter. As he reached for his ticket, I left. Somewhere in this city were truly evil people, not just bitter defeated old men. If only I could find them and feast. O the hunger. I had to keep eating, for I was barely able to sustain my presence here.

Across the street a woman in a business suit had something for me. It was a place at which several humans had gathered to smoke. She was amongst them, large-bellied with a difficult pregnancy.

When I stopped in front of her and looked up into her watery eyes, she took the cigarette out of her mouth and spat, provocatively close to me.

'I know what you are thinking, kid, but beat it. I'll smoke if I want to.' Her voice was more tired than angry. I laughed, savouring the guilt especially, before leaving her, drained and disheartened to the point of tears.

From person to person I moved through the streets, gathering what sustenance I could, sometimes breaking into a run to reach a particularly attractive source of energy. It was never enough.

At last, a darker, richer vein of food reached my senses. It was coming from deep inside a hospital, but no one stopped me as I walked rapidly along corridors that reeked of detergent. A sad waiting room contained five women, all unhappy to various degrees. The bright, frothy magazines that lay on a table only made them all feel worse, but they were not why I was here.

In the adjacent room was a surgeon who hated women. Taking

a chair, as if I were the child of one of those waiting for a consultation, I closed my eyes and drew strength from his passion. Did he understand his own nature and gloat in it? Not consciously. To the best of his knowledge he was acting for their own good.

The beast within, however, ruled him. O how he gloated that the delicate forms in front of him would lie with utter vulnerability beneath his knife.

He commiserated with them, consoled them, convinced himself the operation would be necessary. And all the while, with unacknowledged rejoicing, his dark soul filled him with pleasure from the anticipation of the fact that in due course he would be able to cut into their helpless flesh. Perhaps, one day, I would stand beside him when he went to the operating theatre. That would be rich feeding.

Even now, I wanted to get up and take a seat in the office with him as he talked to each of the women, to watch their faces and his. Were I at full strength, this would be an easy matter. For the moment, though, I could not bend their will to mine. Instead I sucked up all the hate I could from where I was sitting, near his office door.

All too soon it came to an end. Carefully locking the door behind him, the surgeon came out of his room to the now empty waiting area. He was a thin man, whose suit hung on his pale form like on a coat hanger. When our eyes met he scowled and looked as though he was about to speak. Speak then, let us speak of knives and blood. But what he saw in my eyes was unpalatable and he dropped his head, hurrying away.

MOVE

This hospital was a good place for me. There was a residue of fear all around the building. Need drove me on, to a room where a woman and a man were holding hands, looking at two sleeping boys, side by side in their beds. Instantly I was choking. The elder boy had given a kidney to the younger. The woman was crying, but the tears were of love for him and his brother.

I ran away, ran for my very existence. They were interrupting my feeding. I had to get out, back on to the streets, where the haze of melancholy that hung over the city could lift me again, to where I was no longer sucking on poison.

11
A Tear in the Fabric of the Metaverse

Had I fainted? What had happened to me? I was sitting on the ground at the Garden of Remembrance, which was a bitter joke, seeing as I couldn't recall a thing after falling asleep on the bus. I checked my watch. About an hour had passed.

This was getting out of hand. Moving had been such fun. I'd felt invincible. Now, though, a growing sense of helplessness was making me feel totally disheartened. It was all very well saying I would fight the hungry ghost, brave words, but I didn't feel brave any more. It had taken every ounce of my energy to divert myself away from the universe where our band was the laughing stock of the school. As a result, I'd become so exhausted I'd fallen asleep on the bus and somehow had this great blackout in my memory.

The fact that I said so little over dinner had my mum running for the thermometer and Dad offering to go to the park for a kick about. But I didn't have a temperature and I wasn't in the mood to run around after my dad's miss-hit shots. Basically, I was tired and demoralised. I went up to my room early and just lay on the bed, arms behind my head, trying to figure out what had happened to me. Only when I began to drowse, half-conscious, did a particular scent come back to me, the scent of a floor washed in strong detergent. For some reason it made me think of a hospital corridor.

***

It was late, the only traffic running under the orange streetlights were taxis. Two bouncers stood outside of Club Galactica. They were being confronted by a group of young men, shirt collars open at the neck, a swagger in their manner. It was obvious, though, the lads were not going to be let in. Not only did they look too young, but they swayed drunkenly.

'Come away, Dec. It's no good.'

'Listen. We have rights you know. They can't just say no. It's the law. If the Poles have the right to come in, then so do we.'

'Right, but for one thing, Dec.' The youth leaned over his friend as if to whisper, but spoke just as loudly as before, 'We're seventeen.'

'Ahh, speak for yourself, Colm. I'm eighteen.'

A Tear in the Fabric of the Metaverse.

'Come on, Dec. Let's go to Dixie's.' Another voice.

They pulled their belligerent friend by his arms and he allowed himself to be turned around. As they came down the street, pushing and falling in to each other, I kept back in the shadows, pressed up against a railing. Their swagger and sense of ag-grievement was exciting. They would feed me well. Indeed, straight away an unfortunate young man going the other way came past them, close-shaven head, shirt collar open.

'All right?' The one called Dec stepped in to the path of the oncoming man.

'Da.' The Eastern European accent gave rise to a surge of excitement in them all. I felt it like a wave of black joy, lifting me.

'Da, is it? We don't speak Polski here, mate.'

Sensing the danger he was in, the man tried to step around Dec, who blocked him. They looked at each other for a moment and then Dec punched him in the face. A proper hard blow. Even from here I could hear the jaw crack. The man staggered back and fell, tripped by one of the lads behind him. The whole group of them lashed out at the fallen man, kicking him with real gusto and anger. I loved it. Behind those clenched teeth and snarling lips were minds seething with delicious poison. I drank it up. Fear too, from the man on the ground, a fear that tasted sweet. Edg-ing closer, wanting them to go further, I snarled along with them and felt my leg twitch, looking to connect a boot with the base of the spine of the curled-up wreck of a man on the pavement. There was no more fear to be had from him, though; he was unconscious. All the same, there was an inferno of rage still being generated by the rest of them, plenty for me to wallow in as they continued to lash out at the body.

***

It wouldn't be true to say that Dublin is a city that never sleeps, but the quiet hours are never completely restful. There is always someone walking home late, or a taxi enjoying almost traffic-free roads, racing along the amber streets. Full of energy from the gang of youths, I roamed the suburbs, sometimes striking it lucky. A cool taste of loneliness poured out of some of those walking home from the clubs. I followed a girl for nearly a mile, taking in her misery with every breath and feasting upon it like a wonderful dessert.

At last, I found myself in Kilmainham. It was no accident that I was here, for this was where my most dangerous enemy resided. Deep down I had no idea if I could face him safely or not, but hunger conquered fear and I stood at his door. Smiling to myself, I pressed the bell.

There was no response. I rang again. This time a light came on. It took a while, but I heard him come up to the other side of the door. There we both were, just a few inches of wood between us.

'Who is there?'

'Let me in,' I replied.

'Liam?'

Geoffrey opened the door a little and looked out at me, a tired old man.

'What are you doing here at this time of night?'

A Tear in the Fabric of the Metaverse.

There was no need to reply. I just waited for the invitation. The door opened wider and he yawned, holding up the back of his hand to his mouth. When he had pulled a jumper over his pyjamas, he had caused his silver hair to become dishevelled. I stared at it with a sneer. This man was feeble.

As we looked at each other, he began to frown. A pulse of horror rippled through his body. I could smell it and sense the release of sweat, but my hopes were quickly disappointed. It died away swiftly and his heartbeat became steady.

'You're not Liam, are you?'

'I'm hungry. Let me in.'

'No.'

A cloud crossed the moon and we were both in shadow, two pairs of eyes, glistening, watching, waiting.

'What are you doing here, in this world? You don't belong here.'

'Feeding.'

'Do you realise how lucky you are to be here? Don't waste your opportunity. Use it to escape your present condition.'

His words meant nothing to me. All I wanted to do was devour him, but there was nothing to fasten on to. No fear, no greed, no ambition, not even of the kind where self-service hides behind the mask of assisting others. The barrier to my meal was not physical, but the absence of any sustenance. Facing him was like eating air and I grew impatient.

When I returned here again I would be stronger, much stronger, and I would suck him dry, searching in his memories for times when he was not so composed.

***

Pretty much for the entirety of the past five years, waking up to the new day had been a pleasure. What did I fancy for breakfast? Whatever I liked. I simply moved to find it. My favourite cartoon on TV before school? No problem. My homework? A quick move to a universe where I'd done it the night before. Fancy a game of football? Another move to where there was a game scheduled that afternoon. By now, of course, I was the star player of the first team and had scored some amazing goals from very long range. Bohemians had contacted my parents about giving me a trial, but I was holding out for a Premiership Club. They were getting closer, but to have moved to them right now was still a little beyond my range.

This morning, though, didn't feel good. Waking brought me no anticipation of fun, if anything I felt dread. My bed was sweaty and the duvet was half on the floor. I'd been rolling around, trying to stop someone or something. My task, whatever it was, felt urgent, but I couldn't recall the slightest fragment of my dreams.

It was almost a habit of mine these days, to lie in bed, scouring the nearby universes before getting up. As I did so, for the first time ever, I felt a discontinuity, a black barrier, like a scar. I've said before that my feel for alternative universes is like standing in a vast darkness, holding up a lamp. It seems like there is a constant flow as the various translucent possibilities diverge and rush past me. Although now and again, in a slightly frightening way, I've glimpsed the metaverse as static, eternally fixed, with myself as the one in motion, rushing through it. Recently, thanks to practice and meditation, the light had become much brighter. Still, I could only see a tiny fraction of the infinite number of possibilities. Amongst them was this rupture.

The black line snaked through the metaverse like something organic and alive, or like a long dark ribbon being blown by a strong wind. It wasn't really like a ribbon though, or like anything at all. It was a rupture created by the absence of universes. As my thoughts approached it, thousands of bubbling possibilities simply stopped. Nothing. A tear in the fabric of the metaverse. What did it mean? I couldn't help feeling that the metaverse had become infected by mad-cow disease or something. Perhaps, in some way, this flowing scar had something to do with my blackout yesterday?

Imagine you looked up at the sky one day and saw a ragged black line stretching right across it, like some god had put a hand either side of the sun, scrunched up the clouds and pulled until something gave way. As well as fearing that something very fundamental had gone wrong, you would have to question your whole understanding of the world. Well, that was how it was for me. I'd become used to my ability to see alternate universes all around me, to the point where it almost felt natural. Today, though, I realised I knew nothing about the metaverse.

12
Alekhine's Defence

My bad temper and anxiety must have been visible when I came downstairs.

'Here's trouble.' When I came to the kitchen table Dad raised his newspaper as if to hide from me.

'Any football today, dear?'

'No, Mum. That's tomorrow.'

'Well, your shirt is in the hot press.'

'Thanks.'

'It says here that Thomu Rogozen is coming to your school today.' Dad put the paper down and looked at me.

'Does it? Who's he?'

'Who's he? Only Ireland's best chess player, that's who. Mind you, that's because he learned his business in Romania. About number thirty in the world, I'm told. Came to Dublin a couple of years ago.'

'What's he coming to our school for?'

'The Corporation have made him a coach for chess in Dublin schools. He's going around the schools testing kids for aptitude. You know,' this to Mum, 'for once the Corpo have got it right. May as well make good use of a fella like him.'

My dad loved his game of chess. He'd taught me the moves, but I preferred football or the Playstation, so we didn't get the board out very often.

'Jaysus, son, I'd love to swap with you for the day. Fancy knocking on the hospital boiler for me?'

I didn't answer; it was the kind of morning where if I wasn't required to speak, I'd rather not bother.

'You wouldn't fit behind a school desk these days, love,' Mum looked over at Dad with a smile.

'I suppose not.' Dad patted his big tummy ruefully and winked at me. There were bigger, fatter parents, but no way was I going to be overweight at his age.

***

Dad was right. After registration Mr Brown asked those who considered themselves good at chess to put their hand up. Mine was straight and high. Of course it would be; a chance to miss class and that's just what I needed. It was going to be a very long day otherwise, trying to pay attention to lessons when my worries about the metaverse were keeping my head spinning.

'Liam O'Dwyer, why do I mistrust your raised hand?'

'I can play chess, sir. My dad is in the Phibsboro team.'

'Name all the pieces.'

'Rook, knight, bishop, queen, king and pawn,' I came back promptly.

'All right.' He shook his head, but marked the register. 'You six go to the big hall.'

'Jammy,' whispered Deano.

I just grinned.

The good news was that Tara and Zed came along too. I'd no idea that Tara played chess, but Zed was great at it, way too good for it to be any fun for him to play against me. The big hall had been set up with four rows of desks, making up a big square. All the chairs were on the outside of the square, and in the middle, talking to the Monk, was a pale man in a grey suit.

'Rogoden,' I commented with knowing superiority.

'Rogozen you mean? Really? Is that him?' Zed frowned, wondering if it was a wind-up.

'It is, my dad read it in the paper. They are picking kids for special coaching or something.'

'Deadly.' Zed was normally too cool to get excited about anything to do with school, but he was totally up for this. You could tell from the intense stare he gave the visitor.

'Children, take a desk please and put your pieces out. You can be black or white, as you please.' The Monk gestured at the desks, each of which had a plastic box and a board. A great scuffle followed as we rushed to get places near our mates. Some annoying brats from third year got between me and Tara, tempting me to smack them out of it. But a quick move sorted things out; Zed was on my left, Tara on my right. Drowning all the enthusiastic chatter was a huge clatter of pieces, as around the hall chess sets were being spilled out onto the boards.

'Dude,' Zed laughed.

'What?'

'Your king and queen, they go the other way around.'

'Oh right. I knew that.'

'And the board,' the tone of Tara's voice was slightly disapproving, she knew me well enough by now to assume that I was only here to skip class, 'you have to have a white square in the right hand corner.'

'White on the right,' affirmed Zed.

'Silence!' The Monk stood in the centre of the hall, turning to fasten his dark eyes on each of us as he spoke. 'Today we are honoured to have Mr Thomu Rogozen with us.' The man in question bowed his head slightly and nearly managed a smile. 'He is a chess grandmaster and he is here today to find talented children, who will be invited to join a special after-school chess class.' This announcement was immediately greeted with exclamations and excited voices. 'Silence! Pay attention. Mr Rogozen will come around playing you all. When he arrives at your board you make your move. DO NOT MOVE BEFORE HE ARRIVES. He has to see the move you are making. When your game is finished I want you to return to your class.'

'Copy me, Liam. We'll see if we can keep you here a while.' Zed leaned across with a conspiratorial whisper.

'Thanks, mate.'

Rogozen moved swiftly along the rows of tables, moving the pieces with precise gestures, the Monk trailing behind, trying to look wise. Soon the grandmaster was at our boards. It got the heart beating, playing chess against a famous player and I suddenly wondered what my dad was doing right now. Because he would love this.

Both Zed and I were white. Zed moved his king's pawn up two. Rogo did the same and then quickly moved on to me. I moved my king's pawn up two and Rogo immediately brought out his king's knight.

'Doh,' groaned Zed aloud, looking over at my table. The Monk scowled at him, but Rogo was already half way up the line of desks and the headmaster had to hurry off after him.

'Well, that's blown it,' Zed whispered once the Monk had gone. 'He's playing different openings on every board.'

'What should I do?'

'Push the king's pawn on again, I suppose. Or you could bring out your knight. I dunno.'

Before long, a natural hush descended on the whole room, the silence of people in a state of concentration. I liked it. This morning I hadn't really taken much notice of what Dad was saying, but now that I was here, my competitive spirit had woken up and I really was concentrating. Not on the game, because I was rubbish at chess. But on moving. I know I shouldn't have, especially now there was this disturbing gap in the universes around me, but I couldn't resist trying to show what I could do. I especially wanted to prove something to the Monk, whose disdain and scepticism was evident each time he came near me.

The problem was, this Rogo guy was good. There were no universes where I could see a win in the next few minutes, which was as far as I could reach out to. So I had to try to improve the position somehow, or at least hang in there, and get a bit closer to those universes. They had to be out there somewhere, universes in which I eventually won the game.

There was no point using Rogo's reaction to help me find a place to move to. He was impassive, his expression more or less identical in thousands of nearby universes. Watching him stride around the tables, it was clear that whether his young opponents played great moves or terrible ones, he just hammered out a response and hurried along. One option was to look for universes where Zed leant over towards my board and showed a positive response to my game, but that wouldn't really work because I wanted to play even better than Zed could. In fact, I had been hoping that I could move to where all of us, Tara, Zed and me, were doing well. But that was going to be too difficult.

As I watched the games being played, I spotted a way forward. Rogo was spending longer at some boards than others. It was only a matter of him pausing for a few seconds, rather than instantaneous play, but those hesitations showed that he was thinking. This was something to aim at. I could explore the possibilities and find the universes where the grandmaster was pausing each time he came to me. Just as Rogo came to my desk, I moved, to a universe in which the grandmaster halted for several seconds. Beyond the shoulders of Rogo, who was patiently surveying the position, the Monk looked at me suspiciously.

Tara was on to me too.

'Liam, are you doing your thing?' she whispered when they had moved on, blinking, and still half-concentrating on her board.

'I am.'

'Well promise me, you won't affect my game. I want to do this alone.'

'Promise.'

The first few casualties were leaving, younger boys and girls who lingered at the door until the headmaster swept his arms at them, in a gesture that almost put me off my moving it was so comical. Nor could I share the joke with Zed. He was resting his head in his hands, totally focused on the board in front of him and hadn't seen the big wafting motions made by the Monk.

Rogo was back. Again a move, to a universe in which I took a bishop with a knight. Instantly he reached out towards a rook of mine. Then he paused, with the faintest narrowing of his eyes. The seconds passed. Instead of taking the rook, he captured the knight. As he left the board, he halted again and glanced back right at me, with a look of respect.

When he got to Tara's board, she wasn't ready.

'Move, please?' Rogo asked with a heavy accent. She shook her head, blushing slightly.

'One pass.' The grandmaster held up his index finger, 'No more.' He hurried on.

Up until now I had been comfortably in control of things, and was really enjoying myself. But with half the games finished Rogo was getting back to my table too fast. His shadow would loom over the board while I was still scrambling through the various alternate universes, looking for my win. I knew exactly how Tara felt. There just wasn't enough time any more. As fast as I could, I trawled around, looking deeper into the possibilities. The black line that sometimes cut across my concentration and ruled out whole clusters of options did not help me find a win either.

Just twenty students were left in the hall. In a low voice the headmaster stopped to take our names and class once Rogo had departed our desks, writing them on his pad. For the fourth visit in a row, I had to move to a universe where I hadn't a clue if I was doing well or not. Still, it seemed all right. We were level on pieces at least. Again that look as he left me, almost turning back to study the board again.

'Move please?' Rogo was in front of Tara.

She flushed bright red.

'No more pass. Not fair.' He gestured to the rest of us.

Tara's hand hovered over the board, shaking a little before grasping a pawn and moving it forward. The grandmaster shook his head and for the first time showed an expression; it was of regret. He slowly pushed a rook right up to the top of the board.

'Sorry.'

'Oh.' Tara blinked.

Rogo gave her a sympathetic shrug and offered his hand. She shook it.

'Good game,' he said, nodded once, then walked swiftly on.

'That was stupid.' Her blush began to fade. 'Oh well. How are you doing?'

'Jays, but it's tough going. It's not like I can make him lose. He's a hard man and there are millions of universes and he doesn't even lose his queen or anything. I'm exhausted.'

'Keep it up.'

That was unexpected. She wanted me to do well? Deadly. With that encouragement I went back to the metaverse. Surely, sooner or later, a win would come into view through the hazy possibilities? But he was back around to me so quickly. No one was leaving the hall any more. Instead, when a game was over the finished player came over to stand behind those of us who were still going. The Monk said nothing. He must have felt it was fair enough, that those who had lasted this far deserved to be able to see what happened in the other matches.

Every game that had finished so far had been a win for Rogo and there were only half a dozen still struggling on. I was proud of Zed. He was hanging in there, and that had nothing to do with me. I was busy enough fighting my own battle.

Another move, another long look at the position from Rogo. A headache was building up, a bad one. I'd never moved so many times in succession, so quickly. But I suppose this counted as good training for the next time the hungry ghost tried to trap me. It didn't feel like exercise though, more like constantly picking at a scab before it was ready to come away. After each move I really wanted to leave things alone. Except there was no way I was going to give up after all this effort.

Only three of us were left when, to a round of applause, Zed finally gave in.

'Very good.' Rogo held out his hand and Zed took it, looking pleased with himself.

Soon afterwards the other girl was finished; there were claps and a handshake for her too. Everyone was gathered around my table. Like Zed had done earlier, I shut them out by sitting forward, putting my elbows on the table and my hands around my forehead, thumbs beneath my cheekbones, taking some of the weight of my head.

A pawn move from Rogo.

My move.

He thinks, giving me time. But even though I can see further ahead, there are new constraints. His undivided concentration on my board means mistakes on his part are even more remote. Nowhere do I see victory. We play on, the centre of a ring of silent spectators.

He moves.

I move.

This hurts, but I won't stop. Not after having come so far.

He moves.

I move. It's a good one. Rogo leans heavily on the desk, head right over the position. For a long time. At last, he moves his king forward.

With a sigh of relief, I finally come across an end to this that works. There are smiles, cheers even. It's not a win, but it's good enough. One last move, and then I play out the game.

'Draw?' I make the offer.

'Da. Bun joc.'

I must look puzzled, for he smiles, for the first time today.

'Yes. Good game.' His hand reaches forth.

Everyone relaxes. There are pats on my back, applause all around the circle. The hand of the grandmaster is damp and limp.

'Very good.' Rogo looks ruefully down at the board and gives a shake of his head. 'Very good,' he repeats.

My head hurts so much I feel sick, but I'm proud too. It might not have been chess I was playing but it was still an achievement. That's how Tara must see it too, because she is smiling at me with genuine pleasure.

'Well done, Liam, really, well done.'

Even the Monk is looking at me with a certain amount of pleasure, and, for a moment, I am glad that I did the school proud. But at the same time, I have a feeling it wasn't worth it. There are now several more black scars, wide ruptures, flowing along through the universes around me.

13

A Strategy Meeting

There were not many people in the café after school. Fortunately, in addition to the dance music being played in the background, there was a lot of noise and laughter from the table next to ours. Fortunate, because we were talking about stuff that would have sounded mad if anyone could have overheard us.

'That was amazing, Liam. You drew with a grandmaster. Nice one, I wish I had that moving universes trick.' Zed glanced at Tara. 'You know about Liam's ability, right?'

'Yes.' Tara nodded.

'But listen.' I shook my head, 'I really shouldn't have done it. Something's going totally wrong. Where I should be able to see millions of universes there are just these black lines.'

'Black lines?' asked Tara, quizzically.

'Yeah, like rips or something, huge gaps between the universes.'

For a while we said nothing; all at once, our table was silent, though the café itself was lively enough. Over by the door a sixth-year boy was waving around a ticket to the Trinity Ball, showing off that he'd been able to get one.

'And I'm getting blackouts too. Yesterday afternoon, as I came home from school, I fell asleep on the bus and woke up an hour later sitting on the steps at the Garden of Remembrance.'

'You don't remember getting off the bus?' asked Zed, more curious than worried.

'No. I don't remember anything, except maybe the smell of detergent. What do you think's happening to me?'

'I don't know, but we could go see Master Halpin and get his help,' Tara suggested.

'Master Halpin?'

'Tara has this friend,' I explained, 'Geoffrey Halpin, he's a Buddhist. It was him who realised that a hungry ghost was after me. You know, that demon we looked for in the Long Room Library.'

'Yeah, creepy day that.'

'Come on then. We can talk on the way to Master Halpin's.' Tara started packing her bag.

'What, you mean go right now?' I was reluctant to go over to Kilmainham. My head hurt and I just wanted to hurry home for my dinner and bed.

'I think we should. He ought to be told about the gaps and the memory loss. They sound serious.'

'All right then. I'll text home.'

Tara was right and it would be a relief to share my concerns with Geoffrey. Although I'd only met him once, I appreciated the way he had listened to me and believed me.

'I'll come too.' Zed took out his phone. 'You're in serious trouble, dude, and you are going to need someone around with brains. No offence, Tara. I mean, someone else with brains. Our boy here is good at sports and messing but not so hot on logic.'

She smiled. 'I know.'

The slagging didn't bother me. In fact, it felt good to have the two of them at my side.

***

Everything about the bus journey to Kilmainham was as it should be. The weather, typically, was overcast. The people on the bus were exactly what you'd expect: office workers and shop workers, coming home from a full day, texting ahead. So, why did I feel something was wrong?

Because whenever I rested my eyes and felt for the universes around me, I could see that the voids had grown again, had become thicker. They were widening crevasses. Didn't anyone care that a cancer was spreading through the metaverse? Of course not; only I could see it. I felt like standing up and shouting though, to alert them. Crazy I know, but I was tired and fraught. They just didn't seem right, the routines of everyday life, when my world was falling apart, perhaps literally. In that moment, I felt I understood what it must be like to be seriously ill while travelling through a city of people who took their health for granted.

Once at Master Halpin's house, though, my sense of being at odds with the world completely changed. He, at least, seemed to share my sense of fear as he looked at me through a narrow space between door and frame, a safety chain carefully in place.

'Liam, is that you?'

'It is, of course.'

'Tara.'

'Hello, Master Halpin. This is Zed, Zimraan. He wants to help us too.'

'Hello, Zimraan.' Geoffrey closed the door a moment, to unlatch the chain, and then opened it wide. Even so, he hesitated, his body an obstacle to entering.

'What's the matter?' I asked.

He met my eyes, staring hard at me, before eventually standing aside. 'Come in, I'll tell you.'

Once we were gathered around the table, mugs of green tea in front of us, a plate of biscuits in the middle, Geoffrey held up his hand and we looked at him expectantly.

'Last night the hungry ghost came here, to my house, and tried to get in.'

'So, it's true? There really is a hungry ghost at large?' Tara almost whispered the question.

'Unfortunately yes. Our interpretation of Liam's dream was correct.'

Tara gave a long sigh. 'I knew that something was wrong, but to be honest, I wasn't sure about the ghost. I didn't really believe it, until now. What did it look like?'

Geoffrey nodded towards me. 'It looked exactly like Liam.'

They turned to look at me.

'What happened?' My voice was dry and I shivered, remembering the twin version of myself I'd seen in the library.

'It was about four in the morning. When I heard a knock on the door, I went to see and it was Liam, sounding exactly the same as he does now. I very nearly let him in, but something in his expression stopped me. It was demonic, triumphant. Then it tried to destroy me. Just by looking at me, it was trying to suck the life out of me. It was like someone was holding a sharp narrow tube towards me, at the other end of which was a powerful vacuum. I could feel the chill and the fact it was pulling at me, trying to break me down so that I would be drawn into the darkness.'

If what he was telling us was frightening, even more disturbing was that an intelligent middle-aged man was talking about demons with such sincerity none of us doubted the story.

'So, what did you do?' asked Zed, in a hushed voice.

'It needed to eat. A hungry ghost is a creature that is entirely appetite. It had no patience to stay, to try and wear me down. As for me, I was reminding myself that I had nothing to fear: all life is suffering. Had I died at that moment, I would have simply lost this particular body. I've lived as well as I could, more or less. I've no reason to fear death. It wasn't easy, faced with those malignant eyes, but I kept myself calm and that, I think, was why it left. This ghost eats fear and other emotions. You have to defend yourself by avoiding such feelings.'

'Jays', not easy,' exclaimed Zed.

'No. Not even for me, who has had thirty years of practice.'

'Where is it now, I wonder?' I mused aloud.

'I'm relieved that you are here, Liam.' Geoffrey relaxed a little and gave us a smile. 'I thought that it had eaten you up and was walking around in your body.'

'Nope. This is me. The full shillin', as me da' would say.'

Everyone looked a little more cheerful.

'All right, let's do this scientifically.' Zed got out his rough book. 'When has this hungry ghost been around?'

'The Valentine's card was probably the first time.' Tara became excited. 'You remember Jocelyn said she'd seen you early in the morning? That must have been the ghost. Right?'

'Right. February fourteenth, about eight am.' Zed wrote it down carefully. 'Next?'

'That would be the time Kenny drew on my face. I didn't see the ghost, but it must have been near, because somehow it fixed the universes so I couldn't escape.'

'That was when, exactly?' He paused, pen held above the book.

'Well, it was double English, so it must have been Thursday afternoon and it was right before Easter break.'

'So it was. That's March tenth, about two thirty pm. Next?'

'A few weeks later, when we went to Trinity and I told you that I could move. For a moment there, up in the library, I saw it, like looking in a mirror.'

'Right. Janey Mack, but that was scary. Not that I saw it, though.'

'When was that?' asked Tara.

'Mid-April?' I hazarded.

'Yeah.' Zed was writing. 'It was the eighteenth, because we were going to look at games for my brother's birthday present. Around four thirty pm.' He looked up at me again. 'And after that?'

'Remember how an elephant ran into the school yard yesterday?'

'It was deadly.' Zed laughed.

'Well, that was supposed to be the school performance day. Inextreme were going to play and we had shaved our heads. Except that instead the ghost attacked me, tried to humiliate me and I fought back. So we ended up in some bizarre, out-of-the-way universe.'

'You fought back?' interjected Geoffrey.

'I did,' I replied proudly. 'I nearly found a perfect universe, but at least I got away from the ones it was surrounding me with.'

'Anyway, that's May sixth, around two pm.' Zed wrote it in. 'And then there's last night, May seventh, around four am. Any more?'

'Not that I know of,' I responded glumly. 'But maybe my blackout on the bus was significant?' How much more damage was this creature going to do? And how on earth could I stop it?

'Right, could be. We need to keep the list going, see if there's a pattern.'

'Perhaps there already is. One in February, one in March, one in April, now two in May already and we've half the month to go.

It could be that they are getting more frequent,' Tara pointed this out with a rather sombre tone to her voice.

Zed on the other hand was positive. 'Maybe, but it'll become clearer with more examples. Now, on this page, let's write down what we know about the hungry ghost. I'll begin with the fact it looks like Liam.' Zed underlined the words 'hungry ghost' and then underneath wrote '1. Looks like Liam (pig ugly).' He winked at me. 'What else?'

'I've been getting hold of all the books I can that might help.' An armchair stood near the main window, beside which lay half a dozen books. Geoffrey stood up and picked one up. 'This has stories from the life of Yo-Kong Shen, a Chinese Buddhist from the sixteenth century. Two of them involve hungry ghosts. I think you should hear them.'

'Go ahead.' Zed remained poised to write.

The pages of the book had folded corners to mark the passages that Geoffrey wanted to read. This surprised me; surely Buddhists would take better care of their books? There was a smile on Tara's face. She had noticed my expression and guessed my thinking.

'I've had to translate it, so this is only the gist, except when we get to the ghosts, then I've tried to be more accurate.'

14
Two Tales of Master Yo-Kong Shen

'In his forty-fifth year Yo-Kong Shen went home as he had long promised. There he betook himself to a great mountain, far above the nearest village. Later, he told a disciple that it was too difficult to live at such a height, but that the pale blue view of the world below him helped achieve a knowing state of mind. Although he had intended to live alone, a young monk, Qumihao, climbed the mountain to study with the master.

'That winter was hard. One cold day the two monks were meditating in their hut when a great snowfall came and sealed them in entirely. The people of the village were worried for them and came up the mountain as soon as it was safe to do so.

But five days passed before the villagers managed to reach the hut. When they dug through the snow they were amazed to find the monks beneath, completely unharmed, and while the student took food eagerly from the villagers, the master was free from hunger.

'One clear night, when it seemed that to gaze upon the stars was to understand the truth of this existence, Yo-Kong Shen and his disciple were surprised to see orange lights, as several fire brands wended their way up the narrow mountain path. They went to learn more and found that the villagers had carried food all the way up the mountain to a certain cave.

'Yo-Kong Shen inquired as to the purpose of this food and the villagers explained that many lifetimes ago a hungry ghost had lived in the cave. They wished to appease it with the offering that they brought every year, lest it return and once more devour the children and babies of their community. The villagers put down the rice, cakes and fruit, and left, trusting that because of their discipline the monks would not touch the food.

'Despite all of his training alongside the master, Qumihao could not rid himself of craving. Looking at the shivering pallid skin that barely stretched over his ribs, Qumihao decided to eat the offering, lest the food be wasted. Later that night, when Yo-Kong Shen was meditating, the young monk left his master and returned to the cave, where he began to eat. Once his thin body had tasted the food, he could not help but devour everything in front of him until his belly stuck out, as full as it could be. Immediately thereupon, he fell asleep.

'The master finished his meditation, to find Qumihao staring at him from the doorway of their hut. The disciple's eyes were fires.

'– You are not Qumihao.

'– Let me in.

'– Tonight I meditated on ghosts and the ways of banishing them.

'– Let me in.

'– If I let you in, what will you do?

'– I will eat. I must eat.

'– Swear that you will eat what you find in this dwelling.

'– I swear. Let me in.

'– Very well, you may enter.

'The hungry ghost jumped towards the master's throat, but he was not there, for Yo-Kong Shen had used his mastery of energy and was instantly at a great distance. The hungry ghost was alone in the hut.

'The next day Yo-Kong Shen descended the mountain and when he passed the village, he told them that they need fear the ghost no more. The villagers asked after the young disciple and the master reported that he had departed his body, saying that Qumihao had been eaten by a wild creature. It is true that when the villagers saw the body of Qumihao the flesh of the hands and arms had been eaten. But when they saw the blood around his mouth, they set fire to the hut and never returned to that part of the mountain.'

***

'Gross, he ate his own arms?' I said 'That's disgusting.'

'Clever though. The master guy got the hungry ghost to eat itself. Maybe there's a clue for us.' While listening to the story, Zed had been too involved to write, but now he jotted down a point.

'I agree, the history contains many lessons and that is one of them.' Geoffrey nodded.

'Maybe, but look what happened to that Qumihao dude, like, he died.' I must have sounded aggrieved, because a solemn silence followed.

Tara looked up at Geoffrey, who had already opened the book at the next marked page. 'Is that the other account?'

'It is.'

'We should hear that, then discuss what to do.'

This got a nod of approval from Zed. 'Good idea.'

***

'In his seventy-second year a message came to Yo-Kong Shen beseeching him to assist a certain village by the sea. The master set forth with only his robe, his sandals and a stave to lean on. After six days, he came to the village, where he sat among the people and listened.

'The village was burdened by an oppressive tax collector. Every month he would come and take all they had. When they had no more money in the entire village, he even took their pots, pans and fishhooks. No matter how they pleaded with the tax collector, nor showed him their tears, he would not swerve from his harsh demands. As a result, many had left and those who remained were starving.

'Yo-Kong Shen stayed in the village and taught the true path while he waited.

'One night there were screams. A troop of soldiers had arrived and with them was the hated tax collector. He had become so fat that eight men were needed to carry his chair. The soldiers set him down in the middle of the village and shouted for their taxes. The only person who came to meet them was the master; the others did as he had told them and stayed in their huts, looking out.

'– Who are you? – asked the tax collector.

'– Yo-Kong Shen.

'– Yo-Kong Shen, the monk?

'The master bowed, and then looked at the tax collector and at his burning eyes.

'– You are a hungry ghost. I have met your kind before.

'– I am what I am. Are you here to pay taxes for these villagers? Where is the money?

'– I will pay their taxes, but first please listen. Money will not satisfy you. Jewels and gold will not satisfy you. I am sure that you understand that. Remember too that all conditions change, as will yours. Think upon this truth while you have the opportunity as it is the only way to end your deep longing.

'– I have no time for this. Where is the money?

'– You know that I have followers from the islands of the

dawn, to the mountains of the sunset? You know that the Emperor's mother has, every year, sent me chests full of gold to pray for her son?

'The eyes of the tax collector grew moist and bright.

'– Will you forgo the taxes of the village now and forever-more in return for everything that I possess?

'– I will. – The tax collector replied, looking eagerly around for where the master kept his gold.

'Yo-Kong Shen handed the tax collector his robe, his sandals and his stave. The tax collector looked at the master, at first see-ing nothing but a naked old man. Then the truth became clear to him and he understood that Yo-Kong Shen had tricked him. For the master never kept any gift from his followers, but gave it to those who needed it. Nor did he keep one gold coin from the Emperor's mother, though he did pray for the son.

'The tax collector turned purple with fury, his eyes bulged and he began to choke. He would have cursed Yo-Kong Shen if he could have, but his rage filled him to bursting. With a gargled cry he fell from his chair and crashed to the ground, dead.

'The soldiers carried the body away and it was a long time before the villagers ever saw another tax collector.'

***

'Jays', I wish Yo-Kong Shen was around today; he'd know what I should do.' I sighed.

'That tax collector was a bit stupid, though. I could see what was coming.' On the page of his rough book for the traits of hungry ghosts, Zed wrote 'stupid'.

Geoffrey came and sat at the table again. 'Perhaps not stupid, it might be more accurate to write that their appetites blind them to what the rest of us can see.'

'Right you are.' With a quick scribble Zed rewrote the line.

'Also,' Tara came in quickly, 'put down that they both died after getting what they asked for.'

'Well, you say they died,' I pointed out, 'but strictly speaking, the person they inhabited died.' I gave the kind of self-aware cough that you do when you want to draw attention to yourself and furthered the effect by raising my eyebrows. Just to make sure they appreciated that the person who died in the stories was equivalent to me, I pointed several times at my chest.

Zed was frowning, I thought in sympathy with me, but he was looking at his notes. 'That's it. See. When the hungry ghost is here, it doesn't just look like Liam, it is him! It takes over his body. See, Liam doesn't remember those times, because he's gone somewhere else, unconscious or asleep maybe.'

Skin really can crawl. It sort of stretches around the back of your head and along your forearms, all the tiny hairs there stand up. No sooner had Zed spoken than I felt it to be true; there had been times when the hungry ghost had somehow taken control of me. Even then, I suddenly realised, I had some memories of being the ghost. Later, when I'd been to hell and back, so to speak, I had those memories as clear as if they had been mine all along.

'That's right,' I stuttered. 'Actually it's coming back to me a bit now. I wasn't myself; I was hungry. The Valentine's card …

Yeah, I can just about remember. I did go to school early. I was full of excitement.' My voice dropped. 'Full of wickedness, I mean.'

'What about last night, when you came here at four am?' asked Geoffrey.

'Could you have left your house without anyone noticing?' Tara turned to me.

'I could, no problem. And now you say it, I do feel I was out on the streets last night. There was a fight … or something.' It was all so elusive, but it was there. I'd seen and done things I wasn't fully conscious of.

'There we go then!' Zed was triumphant, but not me. It was all very well figuring out that the ghost was getting here by entering my body, but that was bad news as far as I was concerned. Think for a minute how you'd feel if some evil person could use your body and make you do things to others that were horrible. I felt angry, frightened and helpless, all at the same time.

'This is deadly. We're making progress.'

'Are we, Zed? A couple of stories, both of which end badly for the person taken over by the hungry ghost, and you think we're making progress? Don't you get it? I could become the ghost right now. I could attack you. I could do all sorts of terrible things!' I stood up.

'Chill out, dude. We have to figure out its modus operandi, and then we can smack it back down to hell and make it sorry it ever came into this world.' Zed was being exaggeratedly cheerful, to try and head off my panic attack. To some extent it worked. His exuberance was reassuring, and I sat back down again.

'I think Liam is right to be concerned. The hungry ghost is a very powerful creature, and it would have destroyed me if it could have. We are not simply going to be able to fight it, not physically.' Admitting the problem was serious was good too; Geoffrey's measured tones inspired more confidence than Zed's attempt to portray the situation as if it needed some sort of martial arts star ready to kick ghost ass. 'If the stories tell us anything relevant, they suggest that it is not strength that defeats the hungry ghost, but guile.'

'Like I said,' Tara raised her voice to make sure we paid attention, 'stopping the ghost has got something to do with giving them what they want.'

'And like I said. If we follow those stories, I end up dead. Look, think for a minute, what are you going to do next time you meet it? I'll be gone, unconscious or something, so it's up to you. I need your help. What are you going to do?'

They all looked at me sympathetically, responding to the note of distress in my voice. But they didn't have any answers.

15
On the Irish Sea

That weekend had been a Bank Holiday and my dad had insisted on taking mum and me off to North Wales. Of course I didn't want to go. I wanted to stay with Zed, Tara and Geoffrey, in the hope they could figure something out that would protect me from being taken over by the hungry ghost. What's more, I had a new worry. The metaverse was growing more ragged around me, and whenever I tried to look deeply into it, I felt impending catastrophe. Or rather, doom. Each time I thought about moving, I experienced a sense of vertigo, and sometimes it felt like I had already fallen from some giant precipice, into a dark endless pit, my feeble light unable to show me the walls rushing past as I descended, forever and ever.

Poor Dad, he spent the whole weekend trying to interest me in castles and mountains. Seeing that had failed to lift my spirits, they even let me go out to the pub on my own, to watch football on the big screens.

Throughout the holiday I consoled myself with the thought that at least by being away from Dublin, I couldn't harm my friends if the hungry ghost took over. But that still left my parents. It was depressing, being subject to the will of an evil creature. Part of me was fatalistic. I cursed my circumstances, groaned at my bad luck, and generally felt thoroughly sorry for myself. It was ironic really, since only a year earlier I would have said that I was the luckiest person alive, being able to move and all.

Still, learning how to move had taught me one thing at least, which is that there are always alternatives. There's no such thing as fate, just probability. Even now, there were wonderful happy universes somewhere all around me; I just couldn't see them.

In any case, I could hardly blame bad luck for my situation. The fact that this ghost was haunting me was clearly related to the fact that I could move. I just needed to figure out what was happening when the ghost took over and how I could stop it.

On our way back from Wales, on the Monday evening, the car ferry was busy with other Irish holidaymakers heading home after the weekend and even more so with English tourists coming our way. A hen party had taken over one of the bars, their loud shrieks attracting the single men, but driving

Mum, Dad and me downstairs to a restaurant.

'Want a plate of chips?' Dad asked.

'Sure.'

'Here, come with me, give me a hand with the trays.'

While Mum kept our table, Dad and I joined the queue. Just as I was reading the prices, I felt dizzy and saw all the writing double up, like the effect you get if you look just over the top of a pair of sunglasses. I was being moved. The universe in which we were settling was one in which the ship's emergency signal was being blasted out in long blares by the horns. It wasn't possible for me to see what was going to happen after the next few minutes of alarm, but the white face of a crew member and my own sense of foreboding meant I knew I didn't want to stay in this universe. Something really terrible was going to happen here and, with a shudder, I envisaged our pale bodies floating inside the ferry as it lay on the bottom of the sea.

What to aim for? Just normality. Fast. Any move was difficult, though, as I had to dodge around the rips and tears in the metaverse to find a decent alternative. If I made a mistake, I'd fall into those black crevasses and that might be the end of everything. To help quell the sense of panic that had been rising inside my chest, I imagined I was a Buddhist master like the monk in the stories, and it worked. My breathing slowed, my heart ceased pounding.

Having closed my eyes and concentrated really hard, overcoming a feeling of nausea, I located a universe in which no one around me showed any sign of consternation. It remained elusive, tantalisingly out of reach no matter how hard I tried to bring it in to focus. Just as I thought I'd got there, I suddenly felt as though a wrestler had grabbed me from behind and had thrown me through the air. A moment of sickness and confusion came and went. Then we were settled. I'd moved away from the danger, but with little control over the outcome. The sensations were exactly like that time in school when, to avoid humiliation with Inextreme, I'd managed to thwart my enemy, only to have been thrown into a universe not of my choosing.

At least the one in which I'd landed seemed fine. For a start there was no alarm signal being played. There was some dismay among the people around us, though, and I began to sweat again. What was troubling them? Dad went up to the front of the queue to see, and then came back with a shrug.

'The staff have all gone.'

'Let's go back to Mum.' This was really worrying. At least if we sat together, it would be easier for me to keep an eye on them both. I'm not usually the sort of person who notices the emergency signs, like assembly points and so on, but today they caught my complete attention. If the ship sank, we had to be near lifejackets. I couldn't be sure that I'd be able to get us out of this universe.

It's odd, the way I was thinking, because, of course, somewhere out there was a universe in which the ferry sank. My moving to a different one didn't do anything to alter that fact. Theoretically, every day there were universes in which versions of me died. I'd even seen a few, like when I was nearly in a car crash on the M50. Of course, I stayed well away from those. But what I didn't like the idea of was being moved into a universe in which I could not escape and dying there. The fact that other versions of me would continue to live was not entirely consoling, because they weren't exactly me. They were more like twins and, deep down, I felt that my own death would really be the end. I did not have multiple consciousnesses, even if I could move. So when this one ended, that would be me done for.

Where were all the staff? Naturally I sought answers from the nearby universes, even though that made me sick. Everything was blurry and confused, though. Wherever it was I'd ended up, I would have to stay for a while at least. It was impossible to move into that fog without risking falling through a tear, with whatever horrible consequences would arise from that.

'Ice cream?' A smartly dressed woman came past our table, offering plastic cartons of raspberry ripple from out of a large shopping bag. At first, I thought she was doing a promotion.

'Not for us, thanks,' Mum replied.

'Are you sure? They are free.'

'Free?' asked Dad.

'Yes. The staff have walked out, on some sort of dispute, leaving everything behind.'

'Oh, well in that case, don't mind if I do.'

Both Dad and Mum took one, but I shook my head. I wasn't hungry.

'Seasick, son?'

'Yeah, a little.'

'Let's go for a walk, see if the deck is open. Bring your coat. It's cold out there.'

'Mum, will you come too?'

My mum must have sensed something was wrong, because she put down her magazine and came with us. All over the ship the strangest events were happening, but they weren't in the least bit sinister. In fact, they were rather fun and I began to feel more cheerful. The passengers had realised that there were no staff on duty and were helping themselves at every food area and restaurant. There was plenty to go around, so people were being generous. Except perhaps with regard to cakes. I saw one elderly man with a whole plate of Black Forest gateaux.

There was plenty to drink too and, seeing as there was no question of taking alcohol off the ship and through customs, a lot of the adults were tearing into it as though it were a New Year's Eve party.

'Want a turn on deck?' Dad was as much concerned to have a smoke as to my seasickness, but I obliged him. The fresh air might actually help me gather my thoughts, in case I had to move again.

'Sure.'

The three of us walked through the extraordinary sights of a ferry abandoned to its passengers. Girls in green cowboy hats from the hen party were singing a medley of chart hits to an appreciative audience. Little kids had picked up on the festival atmosphere and were running wild around the decks, like some enormous game of chase was going on. Everyone was having a blast, surely not the design of the hungry ghost? This peculiar universe had to be a random outcome of the clash between us.

Out on the windy deck, several people were smoking rapidly, keen to get back inside to the warmth and merriment. Dad took a light from an elderly man, while Mum zipped up her jacket, putting up the hood to keep her ears warm.

'Mad stuff, eh?' Dad looked around at his fellow smokers.

'Best crossing I've ever been on.' The old fella gave a chuckle that turned into a cough.

Then I felt it again, an attempt to move. It was far weaker than it had been on previous occasions, but I realised we didn't have to make much of a move for catastrophe to engulf us. I could see universes where a sudden lurch of the ship or a freak gust of wind shook us. Then Dad was in the cold grey water, face turned up towards me as he sank beneath the waves.

'No!' I shouted aloud and fought back. Though the move was only a minor one, I hadn't much strength left myself. It was like running so hard you can't breathe. Your body is still moving, but even deep gulps of air are not enough. Your mouth floods with a horrible acrid taste, while you asphyxiate. Kneeling, I held on to a nearby rail and threw up. Blackness welled up in my head. But I'd done it, I'd made the smallest of moves to keep Dad beside me.

'You all right, son?'

I managed a nod.

'No offence, mate, but your son, well that's some terrible smell. He's wrecked the gaff and there's no one around to clean up is there?' The elderly man was cross. But I was so happy I just crawled inside, laughing.

16
The Demon and the Maiden

As soon as we got home from the trip to Wales, I went to my room early, completely exhausted. Lying in my bed, I felt the universes whirling around me, with the dark tears between them noticeably wider than this morning. Nearly half of the metaverse was completely black; it was a terrible pool, which was spreading out to engulf me, no matter how fast I sought to struggle free.

The Demon and the Maiden

***

With my return to the world of human beings came hunger. I was always hungry. At last, though, I had the power to break all whom I met. No longer was I dependent on the flows of energy that came my way from passers-by. Now I could feast on whomever I chose and with that thought came an awareness of a place, not too far away, where I could eat with particular satisfaction. After a fifteen-minute run, with barely a pause to draw upon the meagre offerings of the humans I overtook, I was at the house I sought.

The doorbell sang out its two notes for me.

'Liam! You're back! You should have rung. I wasn't expecting you.'

At the sound of her voice, I felt a surge from the boy. He loved her and nearly threw me aside. But I forced him back down: down, down in to the realms inhabited only by demons. It would not be long now until I had enough energy to thrust him away forever and seal him there, fully enjoying his body as my own.

Embarrassment is pleasure and nourishment to me. With a slight sneer on my face, I let her see me slowly move my gaze up and down, observing the pink hoody, the pink tracksuit bottoms and a pale line of chubby skin between them. She blushed, and pulled at her top. There was nothing she could do to hide the false foot though, which I stared at for some time.

'I was just going to take Rascal for a walk. Want to come along?'

'I do.'

'Rascal? Walkies!'

The dog feared me. It wanted to be brave and protect her, but fear was winning.

'Rascal, come on!'

With a whimper, the dog allowed itself to be collared and, staying away from me as far as possible, it slunk from the house.

'He normally really loves to get out.'

There was a great deal of affection and concern flowing from her in my direction; it was unpalatable, almost poisonous to me and I strove to ignore it. At least the suburbs were good hunting grounds. Already we had passed two young humans in a lane: him, a bonfire of lust and contempt; her, lust and guilt. It was heady and I drew upon it with relish.

'I've been thinking about those stories Geoffrey told us. It would be great if he could find some more. I think we've gained a lot, just from those two.'

It wasn't her eager chat that I was listening to, but her heart and her mind. To feast upon her would not be easy. For a young human she was surprisingly tight, like a clam, but there were cracks through which I could prise my way to her soft insides.

'You were a fool, playing on the barge like that. It's not just your life you've ruined, but everyone's, especially your mother's.'

'What?'

She stopped. We stared at each other, standing on slabs of broken paving beside a damp grey wall. The dog tried to growl, but when it met my eyes, the growl turned into a whine.

'Your mother is suffocating you, but it's your own fault. How could you show ingratitude to her, after all the time and money she has given to making your life as full as possible? Don't you appreciate all her sacrifices?'

'It's you, isn't it? The ghost.' She was nearly as afraid as the dog was. 'Your eyes. It's true, about the eyes.'

'Listen to me! You'll never love or be loved. That's the cost of your fooling around on the boat. Your bones will grow cold alone. Yes people will display consideration, but they won't love the girl you really are, because they've never seen her and never will see her. All they will see is a plastic foot and a poor injured girl. Forget about children, forget about a husband. Boyfriends, yes, but what kind of sick boy wants a girl like you? Answer: those who can't get a fully formed girl. The rejects and the help-less, equally deformed in their own way, but on the inside. You could never love them, so you are caught. Be pitied or do the pitying, but never a match.'

At first, I made some progress. She began to open, a tear com-ing to her eyes, but slowly she composed herself, forcing me out.

'Come on, Rascal.'

She tugged at the lead and turned back towards her house, moving at a brisk limp.

Very well, if the thin blade had not worked. I would try the hammer.

'You love your dog.' It was a statement. 'Shame that he does not love you enough.' She could move fast. I had to trot to keep up. A flick of my foot sent the terrier into the wall and I pounced on it, pinning it by the throat, its feet scrabbling for purchase on the pavement.

'What are you doing? Let go of him!'

Good, she was terrified.

The dog gave up, no longer even whimpering, limp in my hand, while a stream of urine flowed to the gutter. We looked at each other a long time, the dog and I. The dog could not name its fear, but felt it as a dark shadow, filling its world like a bank of cloud covering the sky. When I stood up the dog was dead.

'Rascal? Oh my God, you've killed him!'

She was crying, bent over the limp body and already I could fill myself on her sorrow and loneliness. Fill myself? Never. It was not possible. But the juice tasted good. Succulent human feelings were far more satisfying than those of animals. Since she was bent down over the dog, it was easy for me to grab her by the throat and press her against the wall. Her legs slipped from under her, and her pink cotton tracksuit bottoms were now soaked and dirty from the last emissions of her pet. Would she wet herself with fear also? A touch of shame would be a pleasant addition to the fear I was consuming. Horror, shame and sorrow. It was a joy to be alive again and what's more, young.

When I eased the pressure on her throat she broke and ran. Exactly as I had hoped. Eating a human being was not like eating a dog. There was a lot more to unravel. Right now I had a hook to her insides, wounded and raw. The more she ran, the more she weakened, me a step or two behind her the slapping of my feet just loud enough to keep spurring her on, in her clanky way. The rather pathetic imbalance to her motion made me chuckle.

Across the road we ran, heedless of traffic, past a chip shop. For a moment, she paused. Would she seek out other human beings? Yes. In she went, panting, cold, afraid, heartbeat already dangerously erratic.

Four young girls, dressed in loud primary colours, were waiting for their food. They had been laughing and shouting as we came in. Now they fell silent and stared.

Tearstained and in odorous tracksuit bottoms, she was a mess, and she was aware of it from the silver reflections of the counter.

'Call the police. He's trying to kill me. He killed my dog,' she panted.

This immediately made them all afraid too, I was gobbling as fast as I could and there was more coming all the while, especially when I turned my gaze upon them. The smallest and bravest of them got a pink phone out of her pocket.

'Drop it.'

The phone clattered on the shiny white tiles.

Without looking, I reached behind me and turned the sign in the door window from 'open' to 'closed'. This number of young human beings was good, manageable. Five inexperienced girls and a boy not much older; he was standing behind the counter, mouth open.

'Turn up the cookers, all of them. All the way.' He succumbed and moved around the room to obey me.

'Who has a match?' This I asked aloud to help them

understand what lay ahead. Before I left their burnt bodies here, I wanted to have devoured them completely and thus I needed their limited imaginations to anticipate the horror.

'Help,' whispered the oldest of the girls, about twelve years I would guess.

'Stand still,' I told her and turned back to my real target. 'See what you've done? You've destroyed these children too.'

'Don't listen to him. Don't be afraid.'

I laughed aloud, this from a girl whose fear was a palpable wave of energy coming towards me with every erratic beat of her heart.

The windows of the chip shop were all steamed over; the cheeks and foreheads of everyone in the room were shiny. As the sound of the bubbling fat grew louder, a smell of burning filled the room. Did they get it now? Was their initial horror at my presence giving way to a more specific fear: that of dying here, in an inferno of oil and smoke?

'Let them go!' she shouted at me, making me laugh again. This really was the best fun I'd had in such a very long time.

It surprised me when she found the will to hurl herself at me. As we struggled, she opened the door and the cold air was a shock.

'Run. Get out!'

This time they responded. I lost them. O untimely escape! Bring me back my food! For several moments I was gasping for energy and the boy within me moved.

Start all over once more. There was anger and fear to feast on from my pink quarry. Off she went again, with a brisk lopsided run across the street. It was easy to keep up.

'Where are you going?' I scoffed, all the while drawing her energy out of her. It would take time, but I was confident that eventually, like her dog, she would collapse and be found cold and dead in the gutter.

The chase took us around the back of a community centre, where I was tempted to stop and enjoy the shame and revulsion of a boy being made to eat a worm by his older brother. It seemed as though she were going to head off across the dark field; I decided to follow. There, far from anyone else, in the gathering shadows, we stopped. Her panting was heavy for a moment, and then it became less ragged.

Just before I came up with new taunts, she sat, cross-legged on the damp grass.

'What's this? Given up, like your dog did, going all limp on me?' Annoyingly she was closing up the bright streams of fear that I had been latching on to. Because we were so far from any other food, I shivered a little. Surely it could not be that after such a gamut of emotion, she could find the means to control herself? Not now? Not after all she had just experienced.

'You hope that Liam can see you properly. Not as a victim, like everyone else sees you, especially your mother, but as you were before the barge snapped your foot off. That laughing, intelligent girl, whose mouth turned up at the corners, not down as it does today. You are wrong on so many counts. When it comes to girls, all Liam seeks is the challenge of a new conquest. No sooner has he got you than he will want nothing more to do with you. Nor are you that girl any more. You are permanently a victim and you know it. Deep down inside you know that you must fail in all that you hope to do. Clumsy girl. Stupid girl.'

It was not working. A slow, steady heartbeat filled my senses. It was not that she was ignoring me, trying not to listen to me, for that would be a weakness and a way in. Rather, she was looking at me, appraising me, feeling sorry for me? A burst of energy escaped me in a cry of frustration. This was not a stupid girl. Houses surrounded the field and their distant lights were reminders that close by were rooms with people who could feed me, who, at this very moment, were being hurtful, deceitful, cruel or simply callously indifferent to those around them. Where we were, though, was cold and dark. Too far. Everyone was too far away. She must have planned this. When I thought I was chasing her, she was leading me. Inside me the boy was somehow making his way back up. Did he feel me weakening?

'Your dog is dead.'

Not even a wince. Her spirit was encased with armour which she had managed to conjure for herself. I had not thought such composure possible in one so young.

'You dog lies cold on the pavement and so will you, when I am done with you.'

How had this happened? There had been so much to feed upon only a few minutes ago. The thought of it tortured me: the fearful children in the chip shop, her own distress, which she had somehow managed to master. I had to feed, but I could not feed here. The longer I stayed, the weaker I was getting and, although he was getting ready to fight me, I was not ready to surrender the body to the boy.

'Stay here all night if you like, but I'll be waiting for you.'

I ran back towards those two brothers. Perhaps the young one had not yet fled to his mother, screaming and gagging.

In the Realm of Demons

17

In the Realm of Demons

During that night, I felt a cold black emptiness spread itself throughout the entire metaverse and draw me into its embrace until only a handful of poorly lit universes remained and even they were receding, leaving me in the dark.

This time there was no escape. No point in writhing. In any case, I hadn't the strength. I was being swept down to the realm of demons. It was frightening of course, but even more horrible was the thought that corresponding to the fact that I had been dragged out of the metaverse, something wicked, without conscience, something implacably hungry, had found a way into the light and it was my doing. I shivered.

What terrible crimes was it going to do?

Never had I felt the need to act as urgently as I did now. But how was I to escape my nightmares and stop the demon?

***

When I woke up it was in a place whose unnatural sky was a lurid purple, like the clouds of a thunderstorm at sunset. Visibility was poor and shadowy because there was no sun or moon. A building loomed over me, the front door open. The interior was darker still, but familiar. Those radiators, the tall windows, the smell of carbolic from the polished floor. It was my school. Except that the corridors and rooms were in all the wrong positions.

This was awful, but a puzzle too. The world that I was in was hauntingly alien and yet somehow my past was here. Ahead of me was a corridor that stretched out towards infinity. From the distant emptiness came a clatter.

'Hello? Is someone there?'

My voice was tentative, so I tried again, louder. 'Hello?'

'Who's there?'

Another bang. Like a door shutting.

Walking in the very dim light towards the erratic sounds set me on edge. I slowed, to reduce the noise from my footfalls. Perhaps I should turn back instead? What drove me on, though, was the need to do something. I couldn't just hide. Not while the hungry ghost was free to gorge itself on the people of Earth. Behind me the corridor turned right where it had previously been straight. Great. This world was crazy. The weirdness of the building taught me one thing at least, I was in a world with different rules, a world of nightmares.

It would have been reassuring to tell myself that this was a dream. But the problem was that I was completely lucid and all my senses were as acute as they never are in dreams.

Why didn't I try moving to get out of this appalling environment? I did, of course. But when I tried to slip into the frame of mind preparatory to making a move, it felt wrong and nauseating, like pressure on your funny bone.

In any case, try as I might, despite the horrible sensation, there were no alternative universes that I could see from here. Not one.

There came a crash, like a table had been upturned. It was close, from just beyond a nearby door. How strange, to feel the familiar brass handles of our school doors in such an otherwise unnatural setting.

That was another unanswerable question, why did this place seem so like our school? Had someone created it out of my memories?

Quietly pressing down on the handle, I inched open the door, ready to flee. The room was like our school's big assembly room, set out for exams, with ten rows of desks. It was much longer than it should have been, the back wall of the room lost in purple shadow.

Jane Curtis was sitting at one of the desks. She smiled when she saw me and put her finger to her lips. Moving slowly down an aisle formed by two rows of desks was Mr Kenny. His back was towards me, and his hands groped at each desk that he came to. Something was wrong with Mr Kenny. He waved his arms about above the seats, before moving to the next pair of tables. There was not far to go before he would come to Jane.

Gathering up her pencil case and the papers on her desk, Jane created a rustling sound. Mr Kenny immediately lunged towards her, knocking a desk flying with a loud clatter, staggering as he did so.

A little, uncharacteristic, teasing giggle came from Jane as she skipped away from his splayed hands, before moving, swiftly but with delicacy and in complete silence, to a desk on the other side of the room. When I opened the door wider, so as to keep her in sight, it gave a slight scrape. Mr Kenny immediately turned around.

'Who's there?'

Eagerly but clumsily, he began lurching in my direction. As he passed through one of the patches of purple light created by the hall's great windows, I saw his face. It was eyeless. Just hollow sockets, deep-set in pallid cheeks.

'Who's there?' His voice was angry now.

Not pausing to pull the door shut, I turned and ran, my footsteps far too loud and filling the corridors with echoes.

'Who's there?' A bellow resounding around me as Kenny reached the door. Once I had reached the corner at which the corridor turned I paused, breathing hard, heartbeat loud in my ears. Would he follow? I had to see. I couldn't bear to run off, not knowing if he was still behind me or if he had stopped.

It was difficult to make him out in the dim light and I was grateful I did not have to look at that ruined face again, but he was there, standing outside the door. Silence quickly returned to the building as we both waited. Eventually the door closed again. Had he gone back inside the room? I thought so, but the light was so dingy that it was hard to be completely sure. Was that clump of shadow in the angle of floor and wall moving? Was he stealthily creeping up on me? For what purpose? Best not stay to find out.

For over an hour I hurried through the cold school corridors, trying to find a door that would lead me outside. It was impossible to keep my footsteps quiet, because the polished stone floor magnified them. If I wanted to limit the sound, I had to slow down and move on tiptoe. From time to time, I did this, always keeping a glance back at the way I'd came.

Just as I was considering whether to try smashing a window in order to climb out of the labyrinthine school, I heard distinct footsteps from ahead of me. They were strong, confident strides and growing louder.

From the comparative safety of a junction, I peeked around the edge of wall, ready to flee. Christ, but this creepy version of school was making me sick with fear. Surely, though, this was not the eyeless Mr Kenny? No, the figure walking swiftly and confidently up the corridor was our headmaster, the Monk.

Careful not to make a sound, my face screwed up with concentration, I backed away from the junction, and then turned on my toes to rush away as quickly as I could without slapping my feet down. But the corridor had changed again and as I came around a corner, it was a straight in to a dead end, whose only exit was a door. The Monk's metronomic steps were coming closer, still in my direction. I nipped to the door, quietly opened it and slipped inside, just before he turned the corner. It was my third-year classroom, one we'd once decorated with our own paintings of the faces of a deck of cards. Then they had seemed colourful and merry, but now there was something sinister about these open-mouthed faces. O my racing heart, calm, calm; I must breathe.

I searched for somewhere to hide, terrified of the steps that were relentlessly coming towards me. Only the cupboard against the wall behind the teacher's desk was large enough. I crawled into it, pulling the cupboard door shut behind me just as I heard the classroom door swing open.

Hugging my knees to my chest, I felt my eyes fill with tears. One step, another. The Monk was inside the classroom, but he had stopped. What was he doing? If humans, like mice, could die of the overexertion of their hearts, I would have expired right there. He must have known I was in the cupboard, just from the noisy beat of my pulse. Another step, and then a brushing sound. Was he sitting down?

'Forty-three. Forty-four.' The Monk's voice was cold, severe. 'Forty-five. Quite a record, don't you think Mr O'Dwyer?'

Oh Jaysus, he knew about Michael Clarke. What was I in for? Now that he'd spoken, I found I had some life in me after all. Whatever was about to happen, I wasn't going to stay grovelling in this hole. The boot that I gave the door was supposed to be followed by my leaping out, but unfortunately I hadn't reckoned in it bouncing back, slamming me in the shins and my panicked exit from the cupboard was a mess of arms, legs and pain.

Sitting on the desk, examining his fingers, was the Monk. As ever he was tall and bearded, but additionally he now had a sinister dark light in his eyes.

'Welcome back, Mr O'Dwyer.'

He licked his lips before glancing down at the desk he was sitting on, to where his finger was tracing the word 'Arsenal' that I had once scratched deep into it. I didn't reply, but instead got to my feet and began to edge along the wall towards the door.

When he stood up I ran for it. A fire ran down my right arm and I was stuck. His fingers were talons gripping me so tight that they had pierced my skin; blood was running down to drip from my fingers and splash on the floor. Those claws were iron and the pain was excruciating.

'I'm going to eat you, slowly, your limbs first.' His was a smile of shark's teeth. 'The first time is always the best. Then do you know what will happen?'

The agony of trying to wrench free of his grip caused me to cry aloud.

'Then you will come again and I will find you again. And again. And again. More times will you be devoured than there are leaves on trees.' He chuckled. 'After which, there are other demons looking forward to meeting you.'

'Demons?' The question came with a shriek of pain.

'Those who have been particularly wicked in life come here in death and are ours to play with.'

'Am I dead? I didn't die. And I wasn't that wicked, was I?'

Instead of answering, he ran a black tongue over his lips before catching a drop of my blood on a talon and sucking it with relish.

'Poison!'

Releasing me, he threw himself to the ground, rolling around, coughing and vomiting. With each spasm I heard children's voices, as though he were disgorging a playground.

'Poison. No, you are not dead. Not dead. Not dead.' The Monk's voice fell to a whisper, his expression one of baleful fury.

I was about to run out of the room, when I had a thought. Still nervous, I nevertheless forced myself to step towards the quivering body of the headmaster. By his fierce expression he wanted to intimidate me, but I could see the fear in his eyes. The blood was rapidly drying on my hand, but I reached out towards him and he writhed, jerking his enfeebled body in an effort to get away from my touch.

Now it was me chasing him and I found myself unexpectedly laughing with the relief of my pent-up fear. It was a bitter laugh, though, full of pain. Knocking desks aside as he tried to crawl away, I pursued him to the corner of the classroom. The faces on the wall watched with expressions of horror.

'Go back to where you belong!' The demon shouted in terror, holding its arms before it. 'You shouldn't be here!'

There was little of the Monk left now, the image of the

headmaster, which must have somehow been drawn from my thoughts, had melted, revealing a horrific monster, something like the hungry ghost in the book, all bloated stomach and sharp claws.

When I thrust my bloody hand at him he blocked it with his arm, except that the resistance to my blow withered away. His skin broke open, spraying the air with millions of tiny flies. My hand passed through bone and on to his face which also broke apart, a howl of fear and frustration abruptly ending as my whole palm sunk into his mouth and nose. Those once sinister eyes locked on mine, and then lost their lustre. Pouring out of the slumped body was a sea of tiny flitting insects. Disgusted, I snatched my hand away and retreated as the minute creatures hopped and crawled down the corpse, and began to spread across the floor. With the startled masks still watching me, I left the classroom.

Only one turn was needed and I found the exit from the school.

Outside, a great shudder wracked my body and I had to fight back the urge to be sick. Pain helped. My T-shirt was torn and was stuck to me at the upper arm by dried blood. Still, I'd learned something important about this place. The demon seemed to have been surprised I was alive and my blood was poison to it. That gave me heart. The scary inhabitants of this place weren't ready for me. It sounded like he had expected me to have been dead, a spirit or a soul or something. Janey Mack, but you wouldn't want to come here when you died.

Even though the experience had been disgusting, for the first time since I'd been swallowed by the darkness between the universes, I felt a certain optimism. After all, look what I'd done; I'd killed a demon that moments earlier had seemed utterly terrible and invincible.

18

Untrammelled Appetites

Where should I go to feed? Even though I had no particular goal in mind, the anticipation of sustenance quickened my stride. I sniffed the air. There were wisps of unhappiness floating above the morning crowds, but nothing too substantial, enough merely to arouse my appetite for more. Very few people could meet my eye. Many of those whose gaze ducked down, especially the women, gave off frissons of self-doubt. Was I staring at them because a button was undone? A spot was visible beneath their make-up? Because I knew something about them? This was pitiful nonsense. The stream of office workers had carried me past Trinity College and my hunger urged me inside.

Here the pickings were only slightly better. Less of them were intimidated by my scrutiny; in fact the opposite, there was a certain amount of self-importance to devour. Who was I, a young kid, to be looking at them? Did I envy them? I should.

This one was a little tastier. She had come out of the library exulting in her triumph. The early bird catches the worm, she told herself. By coming in ahead of the others of her class she had managed to get her hands on the psychology books they needed for their exams. No one would find them behind the huge black history volumes on the second floor, no one but her. I chuckled aloud and she jumped aside, shocked.

There were trails for me to follow, walking eagerly to sniff them out, like a dog, sometimes turning back on myself. Disdain, ambition, competitiveness, lust, complacency. Never enough to hold me to one particular person. At least, not until I came to the building marked 'Dental Hospital'. Even outside of the doors I could taste pain and fear. With a low growl, I pushed my way in and ran up the stairs.

I spent the morning sitting among the people who came and went in suffering. The availability of this sustenance changed the nature of my appetite. Never satiated. Never. But I was no longer finding it necessary to grasp at the faintest tendrils of dark feelings. Now I was awake and determined to obtain stronger meat, that which comes from the heart.

Over in the Physics buildings, I sensed a professor at work early. Almost at random, I went inside; he would do. Up the stairs to his lab, where the name on the door was Byrne.

'Hello?' He looked up, curious. 'Can I help you?'

This was an affable elderly man, living a comfortable life, happy with his work, not an obvious source of energy for me. Yet he was human, I could break him open. I fastened my eyes upon his.

'You are making a fool of yourself in McCarthy's on a Friday. They think you are a sad lonely man and they are right. You have absolutely no hope with Eithne. She is only being kind and your fantasies are entirely misplaced.'

At first he opened his mouth, about to retort, but the mention of Eithne's name killed that. Instead he glowered at me angrily. Good.

'Why didn't you credit Ger Singleton on your paper to the Royal Irish Academy last year?'

'What are you talking about?'

'You know.'

He flushed. Excellent, I inhaled heartily.

'That wasn't the worst of it, though. What about the reference you wrote for him to the Research Council. He trusted you. He probably still does. That would change rather a lot, don't you think, if he could see what you had written. Jealousy? Fear that he would supplant you? That he would get the O'Reilly Award?'

The professor was cast down, physically slumping back into his chair, ashamed to meet my eye.

'What are you?' he muttered. 'How do you know about those things?'

'When you were a boy, your family had nothing. Remember crying because Robert McCarthy recognised your blazer, it was the old one his family had given away to Oxfam? Robert pulled you around the playground, showing the ink marks on the inside pockets. You were denying it through your tears, but you knew he was right. You've come a long way, Professor. If your father was alive, he would be very proud of you. Or would he? Your father believed there was never any excuse for a lie. Remember? What would he think about the way you've treated Singleton?'

'Stop it,' the professor whispered, his face bright red.

'Come with me.' I had him.

'Go away. Get out.' There was no force in his words.

'Why did you let your brother fall? He was only six and he was stuck, high up on the climbing bars. He was screaming for you. What were you doing Byrne? Busy with your older friends, too embarrassed to help him? Until tiredness, vertigo and fear won. You turned just in time to see him let go and break both his ankles.'

'Oh God.' A tear rolled down his cheek.

'Get up!'

This time he complied.

'Go ahead of me, show me the way to the roof.'

It is extraordinary the difference in the walk of a person at ease with themselves, and one in the throes of misery. Byrne didn't look up at all, his hands barely moved from his sides. From over his shoulder, I leaned to whisper in his ear.

'How long do you think Veronica waited for your call? You know what it meant to her, a girl like that, to sleep with you. She trusted you. She believed she had met her soul mate in you and you let her believe it. What was it you said? If she was the princess in the fairytale, then you were the woodcutter, poor but honest. That, pathetic as it now sounds, clinched the matter, didn't it? Your evident pride in truth over riches. But afterwards you panicked and couldn't even ring her, couldn't talk to her. What must she have gone through?'

Feasting on this man was good. All the better for the fact that his feelings had been buried deep, unexamined for years, smoothed over. He was ill prepared for them, and for me. There was no barrier between us, not like the girl or the monk. They had already examined their flaws under a harsh light and would not flinch from them. Pure force would be needed there. Byrne though was hurting and I was drinking at the wounds.

The fire escape made a loud racket as I pulled it down, worrying me that we might attract attention and this delicious feast would be interrupted. Byrne just stood there, passively, until I ordered him up. The day was breezy, low clouds swiftly moving above a skyline of cranes and grey buildings.

'Come here. Stand on the lip.'

While I sat on the granite wall that surrounded the edge of the building, Byrne clambered right up on to it. There was nothing between him and a three-storey fall onto tarmac. His death was certain.

'Look down.'

For a moment he glanced at me, the smiling boy sitting in front of him, and then his gaze continued on past me, to the drop.

'In a few minutes I'm going to order you to step off. How does that feel?'

There was not the will in him to answer, but I enjoyed his fear all the same.

'Hold out your left arm. Now stand on one leg, and hold the other over the edge.'

I let out a long sigh; this was good food. Yet I wanted more. Always I want more. And there was a lot more to be had from Byrne. It would be a waste to kill him now. With a chuckle at the sight of the professor, shaking as he balanced on the edge of destruction, I got up. My appetite had risen again, along with my strength. Time to roam the world and, where it did not produce its own misery, help create some.

19

Trudging through Hell

After walking for hours through featureless dust, I was growing frustrated. Did my experience of time match that of Earth? If so, how much harm had the hungry ghost done already? At last, I saw a dot on the horizon. It was a young boy. At first, I thought he was sick, the way he was crouched, like he might have had a bad stomach ache, but, after a while, I realised that he was leaning over to study ants as they scurried across the dirt.

'Hello.'

'Hello,' he replied, without looking up.

'What are you doing?' I crouched down beside him.

'Thinking.'

'What about?'

'Lots of things. Like this ant. Is it the same one I saw before, or another one? It's hard to tell from here. Then I was thinking about the nest. I don't know how many ants are in this nest, but I think twenty thousand. This made me wonder if they are performing difficult computations.'

I felt like laughing, but he was serious.

'How do you mean?'

'Each one of them has a few brain cells, let's say a quarter of a million.' Still the boy had not spared me a glance. 'Together, they amount to enough brain cells to be pretty smart, nearly as smart as a human. What if they aren't really individual insects, but each one is a part of a much bigger whole? What if there's a pattern? These are strange ants, see, they aren't carrying food back to the nest. What are they doing?'

Once he had said this, I turned my attention to the ants. Actually, they were fascinating. The boy was right. The way they were marching around had some kind of purpose. There was meaning here. Even when they climbed over stones or blades of grass, they came back into line, the distances between each ant varied, but it was not random. Or was it?

After several days, I realised that you could distinguish between the individual ants, some of them were different colours, some were slightly larger or smaller than the others. The boy was not crazy when he had wondered if he'd seen a particular ant earlier. This discovery would help I lot, I was sure.

There was a boy beside me. I'd forgotten that.

'Have you worked it out?' I asked him.

'No. But I think it has something to do with Pi.'

I started to look again. The constant motion was intriguing, but it was hard to keep up with them all. Just when you thought you had an insight into the pattern it disassembled again. The ants were definitely purposely, collectively, engaged in some fascinating activity.

Since I was comfortable here, not needing to eat or drink, or even move, I lost track of time. Perhaps ten years went by. I know that ten years is a very long time. But under this unchanging purple sky my earlier question was answered. There was no time here, not like I was used to. The only motion was the endlessly fascinating to-ing and fro-ing of the ants.

'Ahh,' the boy sighed. I noticed him again. 'It's me. It's my thoughts.'

Was it? Did they respond to his thinking?

The ants began to move a little more urgently.

'Would you mind if we ate you?' The boy sent me a predatory glance, sure that he had ensnared me.

'No. But if you are a demon, you shouldn't. I'm not dead. I've come here a different way. I'll poison you.'

An ant crawled over my finger and with its mandibles prised a tiny flake of dried blood from where it had stuck to a hair of my hand. Several more came to me and I watched with great interest as they crossed my knuckles, treading so lightly I could hardly feel them. That was before a new kind of ant came, one with oversized jaws. This one did not try to get up on to my hand, but instead tore a thin layer of skin loose from my fingertip, working at it for perhaps an hour, before being able to leave, carrying its trophy above its head.

'It will take a long time.' The boy **was** apologetic.

'That's all right.'

The pattern no longer interested me. It was as though a cloud had come between me and the sun, except that there were no clouds, no sun. Just the constant gloomy sky.

After a few days, I looked up, the boy was face down in the dirt, dead. Dead ants lay all around him, the last few struggling to move, twitching their legs and antenna.

Disappointed, I stood up. Only after I had walked for several miles did I start to remember. I was Liam. Everything was restored to me and I gasped, short of breath.

'Jaysus!'

I'd killed another demon, but entirely by luck. I could have been crouched over that bit of dirt for eternity. I wasn't going to be caught like that again; I would trust nothing in this world.

***

Not long after leaving the dead ant-demon I saw a mountain on the horizon. I almost gave a little skip of delight. It was a sign that the drab terrain was not endless. Naturally I walked toward it, a cone shaped silhouette against the purple sky. After several days, I realised it was not getting any closer.

The steady crunch of my feet on to the dirt sometimes formed the basis of a rhythm that caused my mind to recall tunes. Chart hits mostly. I was idly speculating on 'Hand In My Pocket', trying to remember the lyrics, when I found myself back in the school disco, listening to the same song. These were fairly tame events, no drink except that which we had smuggled in. The moment was familiar. Deano was dancing with Jocelyn Doonan, who I had a terrible crush on. Back then I had moved, come up behind Deano, tapped on his right shoulder, and, as he had turned, had slipped in to steal his dance partner. Jocelyn had laughed aloud at my daring and Deano hadn't dared to give me any aggro. After standing for a few moments, while everyone around him was dancing, he gave up.

This time I couldn't move. I had to watch from the back of the room, among some of the other lads, pretending to be enjoying myself, but actually suffering from acute jealousy.

'Just look at Joss. She's such a slag, isn't she?' Rory had his foot up on a chair beside me.

'Isn't she?' I echoed. I could see what he meant. Jocelyn was wearing a loud pink bra under a tank top and she obviously wanted the straps and the lacy top to be visible. 'Actually,' I continued, having given the matter some thought, 'I don't think she is. No offence mate, but I think you are just jealous. I know I am. I think she's great.'

'Liam fancies Joss! Liam fancies Joss!' Rory tried to make a chant out of it, but I didn't care. I simply shrugged.

The disco faded and, strangely, the mountain had come a great deal closer. The ground was rising and the dark cone filled the horizon ahead.

***

A small cloud was drifting across the land; it stopped and came directly towards me. When it was close I could see that it was a ball of wasps. Black and yellow, they hummed as they intermingled in a tight pack. The ball suddenly expanded, to form a face of hovering wasps.

'Food.' The word emerged distinctly from their constant buzzing.

'Not for you. I'm alive. If you eat me, you will be poisoned and die.'

'Food.' Repeated the wasp demon with an urgent buzz.

'Go see what happened to Ant Boy before you try it.' I warned him.

The face of wasps had been sweeping down towards me, mouth wide open, with the first few wasps landing on my shoulders, neck and head. Now it swerved aside and reformed, inside-out, so that a large rippling face looked at me once more.

'Where am I?' I asked it.

'You sssssshould know.' It hummed and swayed.

'Hell?'

'If you sssssay sssssso.'

'And if I say otherwise?'

The mouth widened, it had made up its mind to attack and drew the swarm together. Instinctively I held my arm over my face. As the first wasps landed, they stung me and I jumped back, rubbing my sore arm. The demon was hurt worse though, you could see the poison streak through him as the face disintegrated, wasps falling to the ground, brown and lifeless.

'No,' the wasp demon whispered as it collapsed. 'Not dead.'

What did it mean by 'you should know?'

***

A girl was running across the school playground and she was crying. It was Debbie Healy and I could hear the laughter from the classroom that had driven her out.

'Debbie, what's the matter?' I ran to catch her.

She looked at me, accusing and tearful. When she pulled her scarf aside I saw that her neck was covered in brown and purple blotches. Those had been made by me, the night before at Rory's party. I flushed, ashamed. I'd been thoughtless. This was another replay of an occasion on which I'd moved to an altogether more comfortable universe. I couldn't duck it this time, though; there was nowhere to go.

'I'm really sorry Debbie, I had no idea or I'd have been careful.'

'My mum killed me.'

'I bet she did. Listen, do you want to bunk off for the afternoon? Or go back to class? I'll come with you either way.'

She thought about this, 'Let's go back. I don't want to get into any more trouble at home.'

'All right.' I put the scarf carefully back. 'But let me go in first. I'll explain the situation to Zed and Deano. If anyone starts on about the scarf, we'll try and get them to leave you alone.'

'What will you do?'

'Mess about, start a joke. You know us.'

It worked too. The one time someone called out about her scarf, I rolled a marble up the front and shouted it was free to whoever got it. With Zed and Deano fighting over that for the rest of break, nobody paid any attention to Debbie.

***

There was no doubt about it. I was a good way up the mountain. Progress here seemed to have nothing to do with time, or walking, and everything to do with my memories. If I looked back, the grim desert view behind me went on for miles and miles. Twice now I'd come across situations from my past and both times I'd left them to find myself higher up. Movement here had something to do with recreating my past. Then there was the strange comment from the wasp demon. 'You should know.' Was this entire hell somehow of my making?

20
Of Mountains and Murder

Here was a quiet street of cottages with well-kept gardens. Normally this would be too quiet for me. Three human beings were inside this house: the monk, a girl and a boy. They were talking, concerned. I would turn that concern to fear. The thought of the coming feast nearly drove me to attack at once, but it was worth waiting, to suck every last drop of sustenance from them. I lingered at the window, sniffing. It was some time before the boy saw me.

'Liam!'

They came forward. Just a thin pane of glass between us. I smiled.

'That's not Liam.' The girl took a step backwards. 'It's the ghost. Look at his eyes.'

Yes. Look at my eyes and tremble.

The man closed the curtains. Hilarious. As if that could do any good. While their anxiety grew, I sauntered out of the garden, leaving the gate open. The neighbour's house had a garden gnome. It was heavy, with damp soil clinging to its base. I returned, both hands underneath the gnome, leaning it against my shoulder while I considered their thoughts.

Just as their sense of panic was fading I threw the gnome into the window as hard as I could. The leap of alarm following the crash, even from the man, was succulent. There was no need to hurry while kicking out the sharp pieces of glass that remained attached to the lower window frame. Let them listen to my impending arrival and their anticipation of horror grow.

'What are we going to do?' shouted the boy. 'He's getting in.'

'Try not to be afraid. That's what it wants. Anger too,' the man responded.

'Don't you know some martial arts or something? Can't you take him down?' The boy was terrified.

Getting through the curtains was a little awkward, but I didn't rush things. It must have been very disturbing for them to see the misshapen outline of my body as I made the effort to tear the curtains down from the outside.

'Hello,' I spoke after I had pulled the cloth down from the railings above the window. The four of us stood among the broken glass, in a room lined with books.

* * *

Two demons came up the mountain towards me. One was massive, twice my height, tusks protruding upwards from its lower jaw. The other was thin and angular, like a stick insect walking upright.

'Don't try to eat me. I'm not dead. You'll be poisoned.'

'We know,' boomed the giant.

'Where are you going?' whispered the stick demon.

'Up.'

'Why?' The large one roared, showing his teeth.

'It feels right.'

'Stay. Come with us. You shall be king here, none can defy you.' The stick demon waved a long arm, unrolling his fingers towards the landscape below. What had appeared previously to be nothing but dreary scrub and dirt was revealed to be far more interesting. Hundreds, no, thousands, of demons lived there, in palaces, on golden riverboats, in silk tents. There was, in fact, a kingdom, with princes, dukes, lords and armies of demons. It was mine for the taking, for who indeed could stop me?

It might seem obvious that this invitation was a lure. Of course it was a lure. Yet it was worth considering. After all, was a short life in Dublin really worth striving for compared to the epochs of existence that could be mine here? What's more, if there really was no time in this realm, I could be king for as long as I liked, then go home whenever I chose. I hesitated and, without taking their eyes off me, the two demons bowed low. It would be an amazing experience, to be king of the demons.

All the same, I wanted to be back in Dublin. For a start Arsenal were in the semi-finals this Saturday. I laughed at myself, for being motivated by such a relatively trivial matter, I should have been thinking about my parents and friends, or Tara. Or should I?

It came back to me how I'd seen them betray me, or tell lies, or behave selfishly. Even Tara, who was in a league of her own, behaved selfishly at times, or rather, in some universes. Such failings were inevitable; we were human. Considering these incidents, though, reminded me that the question of what to do was a question for me alone, like it always had been. I had no obligations to anyone else, and this made me feel excited, free. I took several steps down the mountain, ready for adventure, the two demons at my side. Then I halted.

'Lord?' growled the giant.

'Master?' queried the stick demon.

'I'm bored already.'

'Bored?' The giant was amazed.

The other demon flung its arms wide. 'Ahead of you is splendour, treasure beyond compare. Magic, weapons. There are wars to fight, legends to create and listen to. There are skilled entertainers who will delight you, tease you, satisfy you. Come with us Lord and taste it all.'

'No. Sorry guys, but something isn't right. I have the feeling that fighting wars here will be like playing chess against myself; that listening to legends will be like hearing my own voice. Fill this world with a million demons and somehow it will still be empty.'

They looked at each other, concerned, but did not dare to try and stop me as I turned around to go back up the mountain. They did follow me though and from further down I saw motion, as if more were coming.

* * *

It was the boy who broke first. He could not stand the tension and his own fear.

'I'm taking him down.'

'Don't,' muttered Geoffrey, desperately trying to keep his own emotions in check.

The boy leapt at me, his jaws clenched, arms raised. It was simply a matter of drawing up all his alarm and recklessness and twisting it back upon him.

'Fall!' I stared at him and he collapsed onto the floor. 'Crawl through the glass!' I commanded. Slowly he got up on to his hands and knees and began to creep around the room, seeking the areas where there were pieces of glass.

'Stop it!' shrieked the girl. She ran ahead of him, trying to sweep the splinters out of the way. It was unavoidable that some remained. There was so much glass everywhere, and after several minutes of this thoroughly enjoyable game, smears of blood began to appear on the polished wood, marking the painful route of the boy. This was pleasant: the anger, pain and frustration of the boy; the distress of the girl. Plenty for me to eat. And even more satisfying was the knowledge that there was more to come.

'Geoffrey, do something, please.' She was crying.

He was still closed tight, watching, waiting. Tight, but not completely shut to me. There were cracks. Inside, his calm was being undermined by concern for the children. Good, there would be a way to break him too. By the time I left this room I would have feasted on the living hearts of them all.

* * *

Deano had been pushing me all day, testing me. At last, in chemistry, he challenged me to a fight. The rest of the class were eager to see it.

'Don't run out after the class.' He warned me.

'I won't.' I should have been worried; he was physically far stronger than me. That time I had moved and won in impressive style. This time he met me by the annex; about ten boys and five girls had come to watch. The vultures.

I'd never actually had a fight before, not a serious one, I didn't know what to do. Making my hands into fists, I swung at Deano's head. His left hand was open and he slapped aside my efforts; his right was a fist, the first blow from which caught me on the cheek with a blow that made it flush with pain. I was edging back, trying to copy him now, left hand alert for his punches. It was no good. He seemed able to block mine, but I couldn't stop his. My face was sore. The crowd had to move to keep up; I was pulling back so fast. Tears of humiliation sprang into my eyes. I was going to lose. I was a loser.

'Get out of here!' I shouted at the others, but they didn't move. Deano grinned. I was angry at my so-called friends, who were making the situation far worse, the sudden upsurge of fury gave me the nerve to run at Deano, grab his head and force it under my arm. We staggered around the playground for a while like this.

'Draw?' I offered, gulping back the tears.

'OK.'

I let him go. He walked away, pleased, his friends around him. No one came with me. As much as I tried to tell myself I'd done well, that I'd got a draw, the fact was there were tears on my bruised face and I felt beaten. Which is how everyone else saw it too.

***

From trivial to weighty experiences, I attempted to remember all the moments in which I had moved and recreate them. Because every time I did so, I found myself higher up the mountain. It still dominated the horizon above me. There was a long way to go, but then again, there must have been hundred of times in which I'd moved. Plenty to allow me to make progress.

A throng of demons gathered around me, watching my efforts. They were all shapes and sizes: some with animal heads; some with horns; others almost human, but for their fiery eyes.

'Stop.'

'Come, join us.'

'Listen to my song.'

'Play football with me.'

'Stop.'

I ignored them as best I could.

* * *

The girl was the next to break. Try as she might to remain calm, she simply could not stand the sight of the boy hurting himself as he crawled along the floor, sliding his torn hands and knees over shards of glass. Although the boy was subject to me, he was aware enough of his own plight that tears were running down his face. It was probably this that made her yield.

'Geoffrey, we have to stop him. I'm going to try to knock the ghost unconscious. Perhaps Liam will come back after.'

'No.'

'We have to do something, Zed could die!' With that exclamation she ran into the kitchen, to return with a big pan, which she grasped with both hands. I couldn't help smiling, although I did not want to discourage her.

She lifted the pan high above her head and came towards me, I could feel the resolution to strike swell inside of her.

'Hit the boy!'

As the blow came down she sobbed, dragged her aim wide of me, and gave the boy a pretty good clout that glanced off the side of his head. The noise of the metal pan smacking the boy's skull was satisfyingly loud and even the man let out a twinge of dismay.

'Again.'

Reluctantly but inevitably, she raised the heavy pan with both hands. From where he had sprawled the boy looked up and gave her a most pathetic glance.

'Don't,' he whispered.

'Geoffrey, help us.'

The boy managed to raise an arm to ward off the blow, but that suited me. He screamed with pain as the bone broke and that helped undermine the equanimity of the man.

'Again,' I ordered her and fear came from them all: where would this end? My concentration, though, was totally focused on opening up the monk.

***

Each time I undertook an experience that I had missed out on from having moved, I discovered myself higher up the mountain. Each time, also, there appeared more and more demons, gathered around me, afraid to touch me, but howling at me to stop. There was an enormous cacophony of threats, pleading, reasoning and simply shouts of rage. All of this had the effect of making me want to get to the top as quickly as possible. Not that I knew what was up there, I just knew that it felt right and if it distressed the demons this much, there had to be a good reason for continuing.

***

Mum and Dad had gone out for the night. They knew that I had wanted to visit the fairground that had arrived the previous day and whose colourful rides were visible from my bedroom window, but they had made me promise not to go. As soon as they had safely left the street, I slipped out. I'd enjoyed the fair a lot, throwing darts and hoops to try and win prizes; I had the thrill of feeling my body leave the ground on the spinning wall; I had the pleasure of eating candyfloss. It had seemed as though there was plenty of time, but when I ran home, my parents were just letting themselves in the door. Moving had got me in ahead of them. This time, however, I had to face their disappointment that I'd broken my promise. Dad was big into his word being his bond, so he was really upset. He didn't talk to me for two days.

***

I took the blame for Michael Clarke being in the cupboard that time. It wasn't so bad, except that my parents suddenly saw signs of my being a bully and they didn't like it. From then on there was a little more distrust in their manner whenever we talked about school.

***

A snobby family had bought a house at the end of our street. They had two girls, around my age, whom the kids on our street gradually got to know and let into our games. That all ended when the younger girl refused to climb the fence to get to the den we'd made in the old railway cutting.

'Scaredy-cat.' I accused her.

'I am not. It's just that this is my good dress. I mustn't tear it, we are going out later.'

'Scaredy-cat! Scaredy-cat! Marilyn is a scaredy-cat!'

Much to my astonishment she burst into tears and ran home.

They stopped playing with us, pointedly walking past our games with their heads in the air. Even at the age of twelve I sensed that this was an expression of disdain for people who were beneath them, so I initiated a campaign of grunting at them: all the kids of our street would snort at them whenever they passed. Sometimes we got the younger one to cry again. This was all very well until the day their mother called to our door, ready for a furious rant. It took me a continual campaign of moving to keep my parents from answering the door each time she came, to find universes where they were out, or missed the sound of the bell due to a loud noise on the TV, that kind of thing. Eventually the mother gave up and I felt pretty smug. Not this time though, this time I let her in, took the storm and apologised. To make amends, I bought the girls a present, and it felt good to be straight with them again.

***

It was hard to let go of the times that I'd gone after Mr Kenny. A part of me still felt he had deserved everything he got. High up on the mountain as I was, though, there was still a steep climb left to reach the peak and I needed to face up to the Kenny moves in order to keep going. My barking at Kenny now ended very differently to how I had once contrived it by moving. For each of the times I had moved, and there were a lot of them, he caught me and not only did I have to go through the subsequent angry lecture from him, I also had to explain myself to my parents, which was far worse. Once, even, my mum began to cry.

***

Then, I was back on that football pitch. Remember? The time I realised I could control my moves. After a fabulous and unrepeatable piece of skill from Deano, the ball was coming across towards me, just a yard from the goal and all the hopes of my team were filling my thoughts. The ball hit my raised knee and just managed to clear the top of the bar. Their goalkeeper laughed aloud in astonishment.

'Oh my God, Liam!' shouted Deano aghast with dismay.

As I stood there, I could not meet the looks of disgust and disheartenment from my team.

No one spoke to me in the changing rooms. But, bad as the situation was, it wasn't quite as awful as I had imagined at the time. After all, no one had been harmed. Some of the other scenes I'd lived through on my journey had been much worse.

***

After I'd exhausted all these moves, I was very close to the top;

I could feel it somehow, even if I couldn't see it. The howls and shouts of the crowd of demons packed tight below me had risen in pitch until they had merged into one great frenzied shriek. They knew that it was very nearly over.

***

Even though the boy was naturally a light brown colour, right now he was pale, a green shade of white, lying among the red smears of his bloody crawl, nursing his broken arm and looking as though he was about to be sick. The girl was completely horrified by what she had done. Both of them were gripped by terror as to what would happen next.

I felt as though I were feeding on their raw insides and I had never enjoyed such power.

The real feast, though, would come from this man, a man whose armour against me was disintegrating all the while. It was all very well for him to believe that all life was suffering, to try to attain complete detachment, but he couldn't do it. No matter how strong his training, he was still a human after all.

'Strike again!' I ordered.

The girl stood over the prostrate boy and, sobbing, slowly raised the metal pan, preparing to deal another heavy blow.

'Wait. What do you want?'

The man's voice was calm, but he was suffering, I could feel the leaks.

'You.'

'You can have me, just leave the children.'

I laughed at this, the triumphant gloating roar of a lion over its fallen foe.

'I have you all.'

***

There was just one more move left. The one that had started it all. It would be easier to slide back down the mountain than to listen to Tara's screams. But I was determined not to lose any ground. Plus, I'd learned that facing up to my fears was not as terrible as the slow but persistent harm that had resulted from avoiding them. To the barge then.

Tara looked so young. Her eyes were locked on to mine, two glistening stars in a white face. We were slowly drifting past each other as the momentum of the barge carried it on, all the while grinding against bone and flesh with a sound so ugly that no horror film has succeeded in capturing it.

This time, instead of staring at her foot, I held Tara's gaze and leapt over to her. In an instant her arms were around me and she was writhing, pulling hard on my shoulders, trying to haul herself away from the pain.

'Hold still.'

There were screams and shouts from all around us.

'Hold still. It will be over soon. And it will be all right. Really. Everything will be all right.' I meant it too. I wasn't referring to her foot. That was gone. But to her life. To our life. The utter conviction in my voice got through to her. There were no screams and we looked at each other again, face-to-face, tears pouring down our cheeks.

* * *

This time when I returned to the mountain, it was with the absolute conviction that the world I had been travelling through was of my own making. My memories returned in full lucidity. With understanding came the knowledge that all the times the hungry ghost had taken over my body, it had done so because the worst and most cowardly part of my own being had given it strength. All the time I had been damaging the walls of the metaverse, I had let it get a greater and greater purchase on me and it was by displacing me that it could escape the demon realms and enter the physical universe. As it had gained mastery over me, I had been thrust down, still alive, into the great crevasses of darkness between universes, outside of space and time. This I now understood and all the memories of my body during the time the hungry ghost had controlled me were now mine.

Most importantly of all, I knew how to defeat the demon. All the years I'd been moving, I had been damaging the metaverse and leaving behind a whole range of dark emotions from which the hungry ghost drew its energy. By reliving and accepting all those experiences, I had absorbed those emotions into my memory and had closed the ruptures in the fabric of the metaverse.

A beautiful golden light poured through my mind and rushed to the horizon, obliterating everything: the demons; the plains;

the mountain; and along with them all the fear, jealousy, anger and shame I had avoided by moving, only to let it accumulate in the torn parts of the metaverse. I let go of it all. I freed myself and as I did so, the wounds of the metaverse sealed themselves tight.

***

'Pick up that shard of glass.' I was going to have him cut their throats, then his own. Between each death, there would be an ocean of fear and horror for me to drink.

As he bent down, I felt a terrible constraint come over me. Somewhere a million trees had risen from the ground and re-rooted themselves; an implosion had sucked back into itself all the devastating energy of an earlier explosion. I was trapped, cut off from the cold tears and spaces of the metaverse, which had once been mine to live in.

Worse, I was no longer hungry. I was full, too full. I felt sick and bloated. All the horror around me that I was feeding on was pouring into me, with nowhere to go. I could feel myself swelling. I had to stop eating, but I could not, it was not in my nature.

'Stop,' I groaned at the girl, bending over as I did so.

She put the pan down, but it was too late, all three of them were open and raw, and irresistible. On and on I filled myself, knowing that I could not contain it all. Where had that cold vacuum gone, into which I should be pouring myself, end-lessly? I was stretched to my limit and yet an unstoppable flood continued to pound into me. It only took a tiny rupture and in an instant I was ripped apart, cutting short my scream of pain.

***

'Christ! What's been happening here?' I came back to find myself in Geoffrey's room, with blood and glass on the floor and three very distraught people looking at me.

'Liam! It's you!' Tara hobbled over to take me by the shoulders and look into my eyes. 'It really is you, you're back. What happened to the hungry ghost? How did you get rid of it?'

There was a part of my mind that carried the faint memories of the hungry ghost, like a rapidly fading echo.

'It destroyed itself. Once I'd fixed the damage I'd done to the metaverse, it couldn't get rid of all the energy it was feeding off.'

'You were just in time,' muttered Geoffrey. He picked up the phone and called for an ambulance.

'You all right?' I crouched down beside poor Zed, looking at his bloody hands.

'Fine, mate. Glad you're back.'

'Me too.'

21
Coda

So that's it. You can see why I don't move any more. I'm not risking having another hungry ghost come into the metaverse. These days I have to do everything the hard way. Like typing this all out. I can't touch-type. I have to keep looking down at the keyboard and prodding the keys with my index fingers, so this has been a bit of a chore. Tara has a smooth, very quiet way of sitting at the computer and writing for tens of minutes without pause. For her, the keyboard clicks softly, like an insect language. But for me it's tap, tap, search, and tap. Right now, she is upstairs, asleep; when she gets up, she will be pleased to see I've finished.

I'm glad I made the effort to write all this down, though, now there's a kid on the way. You see, it occurs to me that maybe our children will have the ability to move too. In which case they should know about the consequences, at least, as far as I've understood them. I look forward to telling them, but it's been good to put it all down and remind myself of how much I learned through all this, not least about facing up to my mistakes, or getting through tough times. Taking the rough with the smooth, as my dad would say.

I don't regret what happened. Well, obviously I am sorry for those hurt by the demon and it's especially sad about poor Rascal. It could have been a lot worse, though, an awful lot worse. But it wasn't and, on the plus side, I know so much more about Tara than I could ever have learned without being able to move.

Actually, it's not just Tara I got to know, to some extent it's the whole of our species. I've seen every possible type of behaviour. Some of it is terrible and grim, food for hungry ghosts, although typically the negative activity of our species is subtler than you get from the really horrible and messed-up individuals. And I'm not just referring to the obvious things, like brutality and cruelty. Selfishness is rife, but of the kind where people convince themselves they are acting for the best.

I wish people could see themselves as the hungry ghost saw them. It might stop them spending so much of their lives being false, or anxious about matters that really are not worth suffering for. But on the plus side there's a lot of love out there too, enough that the hungry ghost didn't find it easy at first. All in all we're not a bad lot, given the chance.

Of course I miss being able to move and when things go

wrong, even stupid little things like not finding the corkscrew, I can't help but be tempted. I'd say I still could move, if I really wanted to. But this universe seems like a pretty good one to have ended up in, and when bad things happen, as they surely will, I'll just have to deal with them the old-fashioned way. These days I can face being sad, or ashamed, or failing, or any of that stuff with relative equanimity.

After all, I've been to hell and I came back.

Other books by Conor Kostick

ℇpic

'The most important Irish novel of the year.'
Sunday Independent

IBBY honour list 2006
A USA School Library Journal Best Book of the Year 2007

On New Earth, Epic is not just a computer game, it's a matter of life and death. If you lose, you lose everything; if you win, the world is yours for the taking. Seeking revenge for the unjust treatment of his parents, Erik subverts the rules of the game, and he and his friends are drawn into a world of power-hungry, dangerous players.

Now they must fight the ultimate masters of the game – The Committee. But what Erik doesn't know is that The Committee has a sinister, deadly secret, and challenging it could destroy the whole world of Epic.

ISBN: 978-0-86278-877-3

saga

Shortlisted for Reading Association of Ireland Award 2008

'Give this to fans of video games and readers of James
Patterson's *Maximum Ride* series.'
School Library Journal

In the virtual world of Saga, Ghost is a fifteen-year-old, anarcho-punk
airboarder, with no past and no memories, only a growing realisation of
her own extraordinary abilities. But who is she really? Why is she becoming embroiled in a battle with the sinister ruler of Saga — the Dark
Queen?

And what happens if Ghost dares to reach into such a world, or to
delve too deeply in search of her identity? Will that lead to liberation? Or
madness, death and destruction?

ISBN: 978-0-86278-979-4

Epic and saga are available from www.obrien.ie and all good bookshops.